BLOOD MISSION

*Stuka Squadron Series
Book Four*

Charles Whiting
writing as
Leo Kessler

Also in the Stuka Squadron Series
The Black Knights
Hawks of Death
Tank-busters

BLOOD MISSION

Published by Sapere Books.

24 Trafalgar Road, Ilkley, LS29 8HH

saperebooks.com

Copyright © Charles Whiting, 1984

Charles Whiting has asserted his right to be identified as the author of this work.
All rights reserved.

No part of this publication may be reproduced, stored in any retrieval system, or transmitted, in any form, or by any means, electronic, mechanical, photocopying, recording, or otherwise, without the prior written permission of the publishers.
This book is a work of fiction. Names, characters, businesses, organisations, places and events, other than those clearly in the public domain, are either the product of the author's imagination, or are used fictitiously.
Any resemblances to actual persons, living or dead, events or locales are purely coincidental.

ISBN: 978-0-85495-233-5

BOOK 1: *THE 'GOOSE-EGG'*

CHAPTER 1

Midnight. Outside all was silent. Nothing but the howl of the wind, straight from Siberia, and the vicious flurries of snow lashing the blacked-out windows of the Polish farmhouse headquarters of the 1st SS Stuka Wing.

Next to the big green-tiled Polish stove, which reached to the blackened ceiling, Senior Sergeant Hannemann dozed. In one big paw he held a tattered pornographic magazine, one of his most prized possessions this winter of 1944; in the other — well-guarded, even in sleep — an almost empty 'flatman' of vodka. Behind him the duty radio operator nodded over his set. Further down the corridor an orderly was preparing black tea and rum. The sentries were due in soon. In this kind of weather they were changed every hour. If they weren't, they simply fell asleep and froze to death.

A long way off there was the muted boom of Russian guns — the permanent barrage. It was the fourth year of war: another long, boring, icy night on the Russian front, like all the nights that had gone before. A grey place in a grey time.

Midnight!

The brass morse key in front of the duty operator trembled. Suddenly the inanimate object possessed a life of its own. The operator stirred, but did not open his eyes. At the glowing stove, Hannemann raised one massive haunch and farted softly, a faint smile crossing his big honest red face, as if it gave him pleasure.

Abruptly the key began to chatter noisily. The duty operator awoke with a start. He pushed his steel-rimmed issue glasses onto the bridge of his nose. Grasping a pencil, he started translating the urgent metallic chattering into words.

At the stove, Hannemann tilted his chair forward expectantly, those delicious visions of naked bodies with swelling breasts and black silk stockings already forgotten.

The Eastern Front had been quiet for two months now. The high passes of the Carpathian Mountains had been blocked by snow for over four weeks. Why was a message coming in from Corps now, at this time of the night? Just when he was about to go off duty, too. Hannemann frowned. Then, as an afterthought, he uncorked the 'flatman' and took a careful swig of vodka. The bottle had to last him for the rest of his shift, but it was always wise to have a snort of the old rotgut if there was trouble brewing. He waited.

In the stove the logs crackled merrily, casting a ruddy glow on the crude mud walls of the farmhouse. Outside there was the weary trudge of heavy boots on the hard frozen snow: the sentries were coming. In a moment, the headquarters would be full of them, slapping their arms around their skinny frozen bodies, noses red, pinched and dripping, eyebrows white and sparkling with hoar-frost, breath fogging the air in grey clouds. At the morse key, the signaller was scribbling down his message, face revealing all too clearly his bewilderment. Hannemann risked another sip of the precious black-market vodka and felt that satisfying hot punch at the base of his stomach. The shit had hit the fan somewhere, he just knew it, as surely as he knew he hadn't had sexfor over two months.

Abruptly the operator dropped his pencil. He rapped out a swift acknowledgement and hurried over to Hannemann, message in hand.

'Well, where's the fire?' Hannemann growled, as the man scurried across the wooden floor in his thick felt-lined boots. 'Come on, man — spit out the shit.'

'Garbled,' the operator complained, touching his right eyebrow delicately with the tips of his fingers as if he were a sorely troubled man.

Hannemann sniffed and waited. They said Schmitz, the operator, wore silk stockings in the privacy of his bunkhouse; and a couple of times at the Wing's beer-busts he had done a passable imitation of Marlene Dietrich, complete with frilly black silk knickers.

'Amateur operator or someone — absolutely shit-scared,' he went on in his affected voice. 'The people they get in the shitting signals these days —! Completely shitting im-possible!'

'Heaven, arse and cloudburst — let me read the shitting thing, will you!' Hannemann roared. 'And watch yer shitting language, man! After all, you are talking to a shitting senior noncom, you know, Corporal!'

Schmitz's face puckered up in distress; then he made a brave effort of it, clicking his heels and giving Hannemann a half-bow. '*Jawohl, Herr Oberstabsfeldwebel*' he barked, as if he were back at the depot in the Reich. 'I shall make an immediate note of it in my personal diary.'

'Piss in the wind,' Hannemann said without rancour, holding up the message form to the ruddy glow coming from the stove so that he could read it.

'*Attention all units, XXX Corps. Forward observers report plane crash ... enemy ... without engine ... region Pulawy ... ten crew members found dead... Footprints in snow indicate several more escaped...*'

Hannemann shot the operator a sharp glance. 'Who sent it?'

Schmitz shrugged. 'My guess is the stubble-hoppers' 10th Division. You know *them*.' He flapped one limp-wristed hand. 'When they're sober they see partisans everywhere. And when they're high on sauce — which is most of the time — Old Joe Stalin could march the whole shitting Ivan army through their positions up there in the mountains and they'd be too pissed to notice.'

From far, far away there came the drone of engines. Half-consciously Hannemann registered the fact as he read the message again, tugging the end of his nose. 'A plane without an engine … with a crew of ten or more… Flying in *this* shitting weather?' he mused. 'What in the devil's name is going on?'

'Shall I send a query, Oberfeld?' Schmitz asked, as the trudge of the sentries' heavy boots got closer and the delightful fragrance of hot tea and rum wafted into the little office. 'The kitchen bulls'll be serving the old tea punch in half a mo. Can't miss that — not on a night like this. Varnish remover!' Schmitz licked his lips in anticipation. Just the stuff to tickle yer tonsils…'

But there was not going to be any 'tonsil-tickling' for Corporal Schmitz this night — or any night to come. Suddenly his key began to clatter urgently. Down the corridor a phone jingled, then another, then a third. Radios burst into activity. Outside the drone of engines was suddenly overpowering. The sentries were running heavily. Already the air was full of the snap-and-crackle of small arms. A sudden whoosh. Hannemann swallowed the rest of his vodka in one gulp, big paw already reaching for his machine pistol.

A thud. The whole building shook. A splintering. A huge rounded metallic object came bursting through the wooden wall, like the snout of some gigantic monster seeking out its prey. Schmitz screamed as it sped blindly towards him. It pinned him against the opposite wall, flattening him like a cardboard caricature of a man, nostrils, mouth and ears jetting scarlet blood. He was dead before the debris settled.

As the first dazed figures in grey overalls began to struggle free of the wreckage, Hannemann realised what had happened. A Russian glider had crash-landed right inside the farmhouse.

'Glider attack!' he shrieked. 'Alarm! Alarm!... The shitting Popovs are attacking!... *Alarm*! *Alarm*!' He fired instinctively, ripping a terrible burst along the length of the shattered glider. But even as the Russian airborne men reeled back and fell in screaming agony, he felt a dreadful sinking sensation. *The 1st SS Stuka Wing had been caught with its knickers well and truly down about its shitting dainty ankles*!

To left and right, gliders were burning, their occupants being roasted alive as the flames mounted ever higher. Everywhere in the glowing blood-red light, men were running, firing, dying. The night was full of screams, cries, oaths and orders. Somewhere a noncom was shrilling on his whistle as if his very life depended upon it. Red and green flares shot into the sky, casting their eerie unnatural hue on the snow below.

Colonel de la Mazière, the CO of the 1st Stuka, doubled forward towards the gull-winged Stukas, cursing as he pelted across the snow. The Russian airborne attack had caught his Wing — and probably the whole Corps — completely by surprise. If he didn't beat the Popovs to it, XXX Corps' 'flying artillery' — as General von Prittwitz liked to call the antiquated dive-bombers — would be destroyed on the ground. Behind him he could hear Hannemann and his running-mate, 'Slack-Arse' Schmidt, snapping off quick bursts from their machine pistols as they raced after him.

Out of nowhere, barely six feet ahead of him, a burly figure sprang from the snow-heavy firs. He crouched there like a squat cat, panting. De la Mazière recognised the typical round-barrelled Popov tommy-gun. He pressed his trigger. Nothing happened.

'*Shit!*' he cursed. '*A stoppage...*'

The Russian's pockmarked yellow face broke into a smile of triumph. He raised the tommy-gun, taking careful aim at the tall, handsome Colonel.

De la Mazière froze. This was it. He would die here in this remote place. He had come to the end of the road

'*Hit the dirt, sir!*' Hannemann screamed.

De la Mazière flung himself to the snow in the same instant that Hannemann fired. Scarlet flame stabbed the night. The Russian howled with animal pain. Flung round by the impact of that terrible salvo at such close range, he pirouetted like a cross-legged ballet dancer and next moment hit the ground.

'You owe me, sir!' Hannemann gasped, hauling de la Mazière to his feet.

'A whole barrel of suds!' De la Mazière sprang over the dying Russian. Next to him, Slack-Arse slammed the butt of his Schmeisser into the fallen soldier's skull. Something snapped audibly. The Russian's back curved like a taut bow.

'Just making sure, sir,' Slack-Arse panted. 'Hard-headed shits these Popovs, yer know!'

They ran on.

A burst of machine-gun fire stitched a line of steaming holes inches from their running feet. Hannemann side-stepped, cursed, and fired. A scream of pain. The Russian dropped his machine-gun and toppled to the ground from his perch on a low-hanging bough.

'Cunning shits, aren't they, sir?' Hannemann panted. 'Can't trust 'em. Not the sort of folk we Germans should assoc —'

A grenade exploded to their left and drowned the rest of his words. The three men dropped as one, the air suddenly full of singing vicious particles of red-hot steel. De la Mazière clenched his fist in impotent anger. Directly ahead of them, a group of Russians were running to the planes, heavy loads bouncing up and down on their backs so that they looked like hunchbacks. He didn't need a crystal ball to know what those loads were. High explosive to destroy von Prittwitz's 'flying artillery'.

'Shit on this for a tale!' Slack-Arse Schmidt yelled in anger as he recognised the danger to their tank-busters. He rose to his feet. Next instant he was reeling back, Schmeisser tumbling from suddenly nerveless fingers, blood spewing from a wound in his shoulder.

Hannemann caught him before he hit the snow. 'What's the matter?' he cried unfeelingly over the chatter of the Russian machine gun. 'Got a migraine or something? That time of the month for you, Slack-Arse?'

'Stick it!' Slack-Arse gasped, face suddenly ashen in the glowing light.

'Can't,' his running-mate answered. 'Got a Tiger tank and a couple of Mark IVs up there already. Makes it awful difficult in the old thunderbox —'

'Knock it off, the two of you,' de la Mazière growled, while tracer bullets swept patterns on the ground ahead of them, throwing up tiny spurts of snow. 'Can't hear myself shitting well think with you two rabbiting on!'

For a long moment the three of them lay there, Slack-Arse moaning softly, as de la Mazière sized up the situation.

Hidden among the snow-burdened firs to their left was an enemy machine gun, giving the saboteurs covering fire as they ran ever closer to the precious planes. How the hell could he prevent them planting their high explosive — and worse: how could he and his two comrades reach the Stukas through that deadly hail of bullets?

Cautiously de la Mazière raised his head. The Russian gun burst into angry life. Tracer bullets zipped flatly across the surface of the snow, dragging a strange glowing light behind them. He ducked just in time, feeling the heat of the slugs at the back of his neck as they hissed over his bent head.

'By the Great Whore of Buxtehude where the dogs fart green peas!' Hannemann cursed mightily. 'I've had enough of this crap!'

'*Hannemann* —!' de la Mazière cried desperately.

Too late. Hannemann was already up, machine gun clutched in his ham-like fist like a child's toy. Whooping, he went pelting forward, zigzagging wildly from left to right, the slugs cutting the snow on either side of him.

'Come on, sir,' Slack-Arse urged weakly, staggering to his feet, fist clutched against his shoulder, white-knuckled against the flowing scarlet. 'Let's get on. The big bastard's made o' granite. Them bullets'll only knock chips off him.'

De la Mazière hesitated barely a second. Then he leapt up and, grasping Slack-Arse, propelled him forward in a drunken gallop towards the nearest Stuka. Hannemann was dodging around the plane, shooting wildly at the Russian saboteurs, drawing their fire. They were going to make it…

'Get in!' grunting and gasping, de la Mazière heaved the wounded gunner into the cockpit. One of the injured Russians lying near the Stuka tried to grab the Colonel's foot. He lashed out. He felt his heel connect cruelly; the Russian howled with pain and his hands let go. De la Mazière didn't give him a second chance. He hauled himself up and dropped into the freezing cockpit.

Hannemann was immediately behind him, squeezing into the back beside the huddled, groaning form of his comrade.

'Time to go, sir!' he cried, ramming back the bolt on his machine gun and swinging round to fire at another knot of advancing Russians.

De la Mazière said a silent prayer and hit the button. Nothing happened. He closed his eyes and prayed like he had never prayed before. It was only an hour since the Stuka's engine had last been warmed up; it was standard operating procedure that the dive-bombers' engines were turned over every sixty minutes in these sub-zero temperatures. Behind him Hannemann's machine gun broke into frenetic life. De la Mazière pressed the button again. There was a faint asthmatic cough and a trickle of smoke came out of the exhaust.

'We're sitting ducks if they catch us in here, sir!' Hannemann yelled urgently above the chatter of his machine gun.

'I fucking well know that!' de la Mazière shrieked, his nerves tingling electrically, his lean body suddenly bathed in a hot sticky sweat in spite of the freezing cold. He hit the button a third time. The engine howled. Face grim and set, he kept his thumb pressed down on the button. A banshee-like keening came from the sorely tried engine. The night air was filled with the cloying stench of petrol. The Russians' triumphant cries grew ever closer.

To their right, a Stuka erupted in bright orange flame, one leg of the undercarriage suddenly breaking so that it crashed to the snow like a crippled bird. It would be their turn next.

'Come on ... come on,' de la Mazière urged between clenched teeth while the engine whined in protest. 'For God's sake — *come on*!'

The Russians were streaming towards the lone Stuka, firing as they ran, their bullets already ripping into the plane. They would be swamped in seconds now...

With ear-splitting suddenness, the engine roared into life. De la Mazière could have wept with joy. He slammed home the pedals and pulled at the stick. Instantly the Stuka began to roll forward. He swung her round. Now he was heading straight towards the Russians, fighting desperately to keep the Stuka on the ground as it bumped and jolted across the surface of the frozen snow, wipers swishing to and fro, a wake of flying snow-spray behind it.

Realising their danger, the Russians scattered. Too late. The Stuka ploughed into them, propeller flailing madly. Even above the roar of the engine, de la Mazière could hear their screams of agony as they were ripped apart, torn into a bloody pulp by those whirling blades. Grimly, carried away by the crazed fury of battle, face contorted into a wolfish grin, both hands gripping the shuddering joystick, he swung the plane to left and right, mowing down the Russian airborne troopers.

The Stuka's nose was a sticky gleaming red. The wipers swung back and forth furiously. Now he could see the running survivors, their terror-stricken shapes silhouetted a stark black against the flames of the blazing planes and shattered headquarters. He caught a glimpse of something through the whirling prop: something that became a severed head supported by some firs, blood dripping steadily onto the immaculate white of the snow. He felt the hot bile rise sickeningly in his throat. All energy and anger fled from him, as if a tap had suddenly been turned off. He braked, then let his head fall forward onto the controls, his shoulders heaving, swallowing the surge of vomit.

The battle was over. But beneath the severed head, the puddle of warm blood still steamed slightly in the thick snow.

CHAPTER 2

'The situation is desperate, but not impossible,' General von Prittwitz announced solemnly, staring around the circle of officers with his one eye, his gloved artificial hand clasped in his other hand as if it hurt and needed soothing. 'Is that clear, gentlemen?'

'Clear, Herr General,' they answered dutifully, their breath fogging the icy dawn air.

A chill wind blew across the snowfield, throwing up ice-devils that danced in merry abandon, beginning the process of burying the dead, Russian and German, which lay everywhere. About them in the fir trees, here and there stripped of their bark by the night's gunfire, silhouetted darkly against the grey wintry sky, the rooks cawed in angry protest of their own.

Von Prittwitz glared at his men with that one bright blue eye. 'We have taken a hard knock,' he went on. 'Gross's 10th —' he indicated the fat, ashen-faced commander of the 10th Infantry Division, whose pudgy hands were trembling — 'which bore the brunt of last night's attack, has lost some forty per cent of its effectives. And Deutscherl's Bavarians about the same.'

The bandy-legged commander of the Bavarian Infantry Division nodded his head, as if proud to acknowledge the fact.

'As for Herr von Nagy's Hungarians,' von Prittwitz glanced sharply at the craggy-faced aristocratic general commanding the Hungarian Cavalry Division, 'they have suffered, too — though their exact losses are not known yet.'

Von Nagy's expression revealed nothing, but de la Mazière, watching from the edge of the crowd of high-ranking officers with Baron Karst and the rest of his staff, noted that he

slapped the side of his riding-boot with his crop, as if inwardly agitated. Still, he knew what the old Corps Commander meant. The Hungarians were playing this with
their cards close to their chest. Could they be trusted now that the whole German front in Southern Poland was collapsing?

Von Prittwitz took his cane and drew a rough oval in the snow. 'Our position, *meine Herren*, is shaped like a goose-egg, conveniently laid on the border between Poland and Slovakia. It encompasses some three fighting divisions, say thirty thousand men, and a large number of quite useless rear echelons — save for ourselves, naturally —' the Corps Commander's face creased momentarily into a weary smile, 'and about twenty thousand German settlers. Men, women and children, sent here in his infinite wisdom by the Führer to show the base Slav how to till his land.'

Next to de la Mazière, Baron Karst, the ardent Nazi who was his second-in-command, flushed an angry red and mumbled something under his breath. De la Mazière ignored him. He was watching the Corps Commander thoughtfully. General von Prittwitz was a very bold man to say such things publicly about the Führer, especially this winter of 1944, when back in Berlin Adolf Hitler was having full generals strangled to death by chicken wire because they had betrayed him.

'Now, gentlemen,' von Prittwitz continued, raising his voice, as somewhere a battery of German guns started to thunder; obviously the Russians were beginning to attack. 'We are completely surrounded after the events of last night, cut off from our own forces north of Krakov, with the nearest German troops to the west, beyond the River Ondava in Slovakia — *over one hundred kilometres from our present position.*' He let this information sink in for a moment, that single eye boring into their faces as each of his listeners pondered the terrible news. For all of them were realists. In Berlin they would have already written them off. The whole Eastern Front was stretched as taut as a bow-string this winter; there were simply no fresh troops to spare to get them out of the trap they found themselves in — and they knew it.

'Well, gentlemen,' von Prittwitz's rasping Prussian voice broke the brooding silence, 'we are not going to surrender. That is completely out of the question. The von Prittwitzes have served Germany for three hundred years and never once has one of them surrendered to the enemy. I am not going to be the first to do so. What are we to do, then? I shall tell you.' He bent and drew an arrow in the snow, pointing westwards. 'We are going to roll the goose-egg like this … through the Carpathians, into Eastern Slovakia, and link up with our troops on the Ondava.'

'Impossible, von Prittwitz! Absolutely impossible!' Gross was shaking his head excitedly, his fat jowls wobbling. Close to him, Deutscherl looked down at his mountain-boots as if to hide the fear in his eyes. Von Nagy slapped his boot with his riding crop, even more agitated.

Von Prittwitz glanced around at his divisional commanders, a glimmer of amusement in his single eye. 'And why is it impossible, my dear Gross?' he asked with deceptive softness.

Behind him the dawn sky had begun to turn a shimmering pink and the boom of the artillery at the front grew ever louder. De la Mazière, watching the tense little scene, told himself that time was fast running out.

'Because, Herr von Prittwitz,' Gross answered, controlling himself with obvious difficulty, his upper lip greased with the sweat of fear, 'the Carpathians are chest-high in snow at this time of year. And because Eastern Slovakia has been in the hands of Slovak partisans since the autumn. And because we are burdened, not only by the rear echelon stallions, but by those damned civilians! How do you think they will stand up to the rigours of a march in this weather? As for our Hungarian friends...' Gross looked at von Nagy's craggy unrevealing face, as if he were going to blurt out what they all thought: could the Hungarians be trusted now that Germany had obviously lost the war? He caught himself in time and fell silent.

Von Prittwitz made an impatient gesture with his cane. 'Do you wish to hand over your division, Gross?' He did not wait for an answer, but rasped, more Prussian than ever: 'Of course we will do it — even burdened by those unfortunate civilians, Gross, and you know it. You have been shaken by your division's losses, that is all. Now, this is what we will do...' He marked a cross in the centre of the goose-egg with his stick. 'Here — the civilians, in the midst of the fighting divisions. You here, Gross — on the left side of the egg. Here are you, Deutscherl, with your doughty Bavarians — on the right... Von Nagy, I would deem it an honour if you would divide your cavalry division into two, to take the van and the rearguard. Yours will be the most important task, clearing the way and keeping the Russians from getting too close to our heels. What do you say, my dear fellow?' He smiled winningly at the Hungarian cavalryman and waited.

De la Mazière told himself that von Prittwitz was no fool. He was appealing to the Hungarian's vanity — and Hungarians were noticeably vain when their honour was at stake. And at the same time he was taking the precaution of splitting the Hungarian Cavalry Division into two. Not only would that weaken von Nagy's hand in case of treachery, but those Hungarians in the van could be used to blackmail the rest into remaining loyal.

General von Nagy cleared his throat. 'I accept with the greatest of pleasure, Herr General,' he said in that terrible accented German of his, and he bowed stiffly from the waist, making a slight creaking noise as he did so.

Baron Karst sniggered. 'In Heaven's name, the man's wearing a damned corset!' he sneered. 'What damned, perverted pimps those Magyars are!'

'Shut up!' de la Mazière hissed out of the side of his mouth; for now von Prittwitz's single eye was fixed steadily on the little group of SS officers in their black leather flying jackets, white silk scarves, their peaked caps adorned with the silver Death's Head of the Black Guards set at a jaunty angle on their cropped blond heads. It was the turn of the 1st SS Stuka Wing…

'Colonel de la Mazière, isn't it?' von Prittwitz enquired. The tall handsome SS Colonel stiffened to attention.

Suddenly all the generals were staring at him and his officers as if they were specimens of a rare species of animal locked behind bars at a zoo. 'Yes sir. De la Mazière, 1st SS Stuka Wing.'

Von Prittwitz examined his face thoughtfully. 'I knew your father, the general,' he said softly. 'We were in the trenches together at Verdun in the Old War…' He paused, licking his lips as if suddenly nervous; and when he spoke again, de la Mazière knew why he had made that reference to his dead father. 'Of course, as you know, I have no jurisdiction over your Wing, de la Mazière. Your chain of command goes directly to Reichsmarshal Göring and Reichsführer SS Himmler.' He shrugged. 'I am simply a lowly Corps Commander of the Wehrmacht. However, Colonel, I would beg you to give me your support. As soon as we start to roll the goose-egg westwards, I will be forced to abandon my artillery. I have neither the transport to tow it nor the fuel for that transport. I *need* your flying artillery, de la Mazière, if I am to get my Corps to safety...' There was a sudden note of pleading in von Prittwitz's voice.

At de la Mazière's side, Baron Karst tensed. He was a fanatical National Socialist, like most of the arrogant young officers of the 1st SS Stuka Wing; yet he was a realist, too. He knew that von Prittwitz hadn't a chance of bringing his Corps through. His position was hopeless. Why sacrifice the 1st SS for an obviously lost cause?

The silence seemed claustrophobic. Even the startling, ear-splitting howl of a 'Stalin Organ' — the Russian multiple-barrel rocket-launcher — passed unnoticed; no one glanced up as the rockets tore into the grey sky. All eyes were fixed on the two men. Even von Nagy had stopped slapping his crop against his riding boot. Without air support, every man there knew that the XXX Corps would be crushed into extinction. The SS 'tank-busters' would be their flying artillery, the only weapon capable of warding off Soviet tank attacks.

De la Mazière's hard lean face, beneath that rakishly tilted black cap with its dread silver emblem, revealed nothing. But his brain was racing as he considered the situation. Reason told him that he should refuse. There was still a good chance of saving what was left of his battered Wing. They could fuel up and within a matter of two short hours they would be safely back behind their own lines, very probably being feted as heroes; the 'Last Survivors of the Carpathian Pocket', as the Poison Dwarfs press would undoubtedly call them. No one would question the right of the 1st SS Stuka Wing to do exactly as they pleased.

Yet there were those civilians. Humble, hard-working peasants from Swabia and the Eifel who had been lured to this remote, if fertile, country by the promise of land. Could he allow them to fall into the hands of the Poles? He had no illusions what would happen to them if that fate should befall them. The Poles had five years of old scores to pay off. There would be a massacre, mass slaughter. The Poles would not spare one single child, just as they had not been spared by German soldiers since 1939.

'Well?' von Prittwitz asked, his voice suddenly dry and husky.

'Would you ensure that I have all available transport for my ground crews and all remaining stocks of aviation fuel, sir?'

The relief on the old Corps Commander's face was all too evident. 'Anything and everything that is at my disposal to give you, my boy,' he breathed fervently.

Around de la Mazière his officers tensed and stared at the CO standing there white-faced and brooding. Next to him Baron Karst felt a sudden icy finger of fear trace its way down the small of his back. Involuntarily he shuddered.

Touching his gloved hand to his peaked cap, de la Mazière bowed slightly. 'Sir, the 1st SS Stuka Wing is at your disposal.'

The tension evaporated. Everyone relaxed. 'Fine show… Good chap…' muttered some of the officers around the tall Colonel.

Von Prittwitz advanced on the rigid young SS officer and seized his hand. 'Thank you, my boy … thank you very much indeed. I knew you wouldn't let us —' He broke off suddenly, one single tear trickling down his leathery old cheek.

Watching the exchange from far off, Hannemann could not hear the words, of course, but the obvious relief of the officers surrounding the 'Old Man' told him all he wanted to know. He nudged Slack-Arse in the ribs. 'All right, arse-with-ears. Back to the vehicle,' he grunted.

'Watch my shitting flipper,' Slack-Arse protested, touching his bandaged arm protectively. 'It shitting well hurts.'

Hannemann looked down at his old comrade; they had been together since the old days of the Condor Legion. 'Well,' he said sourly, 'yer'll be lucky if that's the only thing that hurts, mate, by the time this little lot is over.'

Slack-Arse looked at the big red-faced NCO sharply. 'And what's that supposed to mean?'

Hannemann grimaced. 'The old tick-tock's in the pisspot once again and the 1st Stuka's gonna be up to its hooter in shit before very long, mark my words.'

Side by side, the two comrades started to trudge back through the snow to the waiting truck. Behind them the sky blazed a bright, awesome crimson-red. The Russians were coming…

CHAPTER 3

'*BANDITS!*... *BANDITS!* ... *Bandits!*' Baron Karst's voice crackled with metallic urgency across the air waves. 'Yaks, by the look of them! ... *Bandits!*'

'*Himmel, Arsch und Wolkenbruch!*' Colonel de la Mazière cursed angrily. Behind him Hannemann started to swing his machine gun to and fro, searching, ready for the first enemy fighter to make its appearance.

Below, outlined a stark black against the pure white of the glistening snow, a lone column of civilian refugees struggled westwards, the drivers cracking their whips, the powerful dray horses straining in their harnesses as they drew their mountainous loads, old women and children perched on top of the farm carts, faces white and anxious as they turned to stare up at the protective black hawks flying overhead.

The flight of six Stukas flew on. The radio had fallen silent; evidently Karst no longer wanted to give his own position away. In perfect formation they slid over the snow-bound hills, the sky a beautiful harsh winter-blue, with as yet not one hurrying black dot which would be a Yak.

De la Mazière waggled his wings and signalled for the young pilots on either side to reduce altitude. They would be safer down closer to the ground. With luck, one or more of the much faster Yaks might misjudge his speed and altitude and go crashing into a hillside in the excitement of the kill. 'A pious hope, Detlev,' sneered a cynical little voice within him. 'A pious hope.'

They were flying at tree-top height now, skimming at 300kmh above the long column of infantry and refugees, dragging their great black shadows across the surface of the snow like gigantic crows. They broke to the right and banked in a sweeping turn. De la Mazière blinked, momentarily blinded by the blazing yellow ball of the winter sun and the snow sparkling a crystalline white in its rays.

Suddenly there they were! Appearing out of nowhere, the sharp black silhouettes of the Russian Yaks were immediately recognisable as they hurtled towards the much slower Stukas in that typical loose Ivan formation. De la Mazière pressed his throat mike. 'Bandits, three o'clock high!... *Achtung*! *Achtung*! Bandits, three o'clock high!'

He flashed a look at his greenbeaks, most of them straight from flying school back in the Reich. They had heard his warning all right. They were leaning forward intently, faces white blurs, as if they were willing their planes to fly faster, not to be so slow, so lame, as the Yaks hurtled towards them at an impossible speed, heading for the Stukas on what had to be a collision course.

'Play it cool, boys ... play it cool,' he urged. 'It's not as bad as it looks.'

Behind him, Hannemann lined up the leading two Yaks coming in from the rear, crooning softly between his gritted teeth: '*Watch in the pisspot ... venereal disease in my bollocks ... crabs in the pubics ... oh, how I love the Luftwaffe!*' His eyes narrowing to lethal slits, his forefinger began to whiten as he prepared to fire on the Yaks.

With a grim chuckle de la Mazière watched the Yaks breaking up into their usual strange attack formation — all abrupt turns, sudden climbs and dives, crazy loops and spirals. It was part of their kind of tactics, taught to the pilots in their flying schools, but there was an element of cocky exuberance in it, too: 'Look at us, you Fritz bastards in your Stukas which went out with the Ark! We can fly fucking circles around you, lick you with one arm tied behind our backs and our eyes closed!' That's what the Popovs were boasting. De la Mazière laughed softly to himself, his steely grey eyes icy and intent, face drawn and haunted, the look of a born killer. 'Come on, little babies,' he whispered hoarsely, flying over closer to those Yaks, diving, turning, climbing. 'Come to mother ... *komm doch*!' Suddenly he felt absolutely, perfectly calm. He was ready for the slaughter to come.

'Sir!' It was Hannemann.

'Yes, you big rogue?' the Colonel asked urgently, mentally preparing to shoot the Ivan posturing so absurdly in front of him from the sky.

'Forget that currant-crapper to your front, sir. There are two warm brothers on our tail, perverts the two of them, ready to shaft us.' Hannemann laughed. 'That'll be the day, though.'

'Can you take care of them?'

'Piss-pansies like them?' Hannemann said scornfully. 'I've shat better pilots than them after a night on the old sauce!'

This time de la Mazière laughed out loud. He knew well what the Luftwaffe gunners thought of their aristocratic SS pilots. The 'peasants', as the NCOs called themselves, believed their pilots were only out for glory, for the rank and privileges that success would bring to their impoverished noble families. Yet in a tight corner there were none better than these 'old heads' who had been in battle constantly since they had first gone to Spain to fight in the Civil War with the German Condor Legion. They were the tops. 'All right, Hannemann, take care of them. *Prepare for action*.' His voice tightened as his finger sought and found the firing button of the big 37mm armour-piercing cannon beneath his wing.

Behind him Hannemann did the same, controlling his breathing consciously, allowing the first man to slide into the black circle of his ring sight.

Now de la Mazière's Stuka was trapped between the three Yaks: one heading towards him, two on either side of his tail. The Russians evidently thought that they had latched onto some green Fritz who was walking straight into the trap they had sprung for him; no doubt they were telling themselves that the advantage was all on their side, that there was no escape for the German.

Closer and closer the four planes came to each other. Five young men intent on killing each other, but all confident that death would not take them this day, but the other.

It seemed inevitable that the Stuka and the oncoming Yak must crash into each other. De la Mazière held on to his collision course with grim determination. In a moment someone must break. Otherwise there would be one hell of a smash.

It was the Yak pilot who lost his nerve. Bright red lights suddenly rippled the length of his wings. White tracer zipped towards the Stuka. Next instant he broke upwards in a steep climb, flashing his pale blue underside, the tracer missing the Stuka easily.

'NOW!' de la Mazière shrieked as he pressed the firing button.

The Stuka trembled violently. A whiff of acrid explosive. A mad, hurrying white blob shot beneath the wing in the very same moment that Hannemann let rip behind the Colonel.

De la Mazière's 37mm shell tore into the belly of the ascending Yak. It disintegrated in mid-air, vanishing instantly, as if it had never been there in the first place.

Hannemann's aim was just as sure. The nearside Yak began to shudder. Splinters of metal flew from its fuselage; thick white glycol fumes poured from its ruptured engine. Suddenly it went into a nosedive, trailing clouds of black smoke, heading for the ground at 500kmh. It slammed into a rock face and exploded in a ball of yellow flame.

'Two down and one to go!' Hannemann yelled triumphantly.

But suddenly there were more of them, eight or ten perhaps, materialising out of the blue sky above. The Stuka found itself heading into a mad aerial ballet of dancing Yaks.

De la Mazière fought with the controls as they flew through the violent air, beaten and agitated by the prop-wash of the Yaks. A Yak loomed up in front of him, so close that he could have counted the rivets. He hit the brakes. Now the Stuka was flying just above stalling speed. Another Yak flashed by him, cannon chattering. He ignored it. Eyes gleaming savagely, teeth bared, he concentrated all his attention on the one ahead. Now it was centred right in the round calibrated glass of his sights. He pressed the button. The Stuka seemed to stop in mid-air, as if it had run into an invisible wall. Suddenly it jumped a good twenty metres, as the armour-piercing shell hissed towards the unsuspecting Yak. At that range de la Mazière couldn't miss. A ball of fire exploded on the Yak's right wing. The wing broke off, whirling round and round as it dropped to the earth. For one long moment the Yak hung there, suspended in mid-air, held up by God knows what. Then, with startling suddenness, its nose dropped and it went hurtling to the ground in its last dive.

'They're hitting the refugees, sir!' Hannemann's shrill warning woke a triumphant de la Mazière to the new danger. He flashed a look below. Three Yaks were streaking across the snow-bound plain, machine guns and cannon chattering, and the refugees were scattering for cover, here and there their heavy carts already beginning to burn.

He made his decision. 'Break off action!' he commanded. 'Back to base! Do you hear, you greenbeaks?... Back to base!' He waggled the wings of his Stuka to emphasise his order. Without him, he knew his inexperienced pilots in their slow under-powered dive-bombers would be easy meat for the Russians. Soon the Yaks flying warily above them would come back for the kill, once they had got over their initial shock at the sudden loss of three of their planes to these obsolete Stukas. '*Back to base*!' he roared again into his throat-mike.

He pulled back the stick and soared into the sky, directly towards the circling Yaks. They promptly scattered. He pressed the button that activated his machine guns and sent white tracer zipping across the interval. He laughed crazily and hauled back the stick. The Stuka flipped over onto its back. Below him the rest of his pilots were scurrying westwards, heading for the new base. Before the Yaks could recover their confidence the greenbeaks would be gone. Now the field was left to him.

'Hannemann!' he yelled joyously above the racket, remembering those good old days when the Stuka had been master of the battlefield. 'Here we go! Hold on to your hat!'

'Hold on to your hat, it is, sir!' the big NCO echoed, infected by the Colonel's crazy enthusiasm.

Now de la Mazière flung the plane into a dive. At 400kmh, diving almost vertically, the Stuka hurtled towards the snow-covered plain. The green-needled controls oscillated wildly in front of his eyes. He gasped for breath, pressed back against his armoured seat, ears popping crazily with the G-force. Again he was seized by that sheer atavistic joy. A wild primeval excitement surged through his blood. Within him an urgent little voice yelled, '*Go on, man, go on! Don't stop now!*' An almost sexual longing filled his loins. He could go on like this — strike the ground, finish it all once and for all … he fought off that old, old desire to surrender, to yield to the seduction of this wild, crazed dive to destruction.

At the very last minute, he hit the brakes and jerked back the stick. The whole fuselage trembled like a live thing. De la Mazière ripped open his mouth, gasping for breath as if he had just run a great race. Stars popped in front of his eyes. His eardrums were threatening to burst at any moment. For an instant he choked and gasped like a stranded fish; then he shook his head. His tremendous dive had paid off. He had caught up with the much faster Yaks. There they were, braking in a tight turn, white vapour trails etched in the hard blue winter sky, as they prepared to come in for another run at the shattered column of carts, the snowfields on both sides littered with the bodies of dead civilians.

'Hannemann,' he gasped, 'keep your glassy orbits peeled! I'm attacking!'

'Peeled like a tomato!' Hannemann yelled loyally, swinging his single machine gun, preparing to ward off any attacker from the rear. 'Give the Popov bastards hell!'

'That I will!' de la Mazière yelled back as he sent the Stuka racing towards the Yaks.

The three Russian planes were still skimming across the surface of the snowfield, cannon and machine guns hammering. A civilian toppled from a tree, felled like a partridge. Carts went up in bursts of cherry-red flames. A bunch of civilians hiding in a grove of firs panicked and fled out into the open. The Yaks showed no mercy. One of them broke away from the rest and, banking in a steep left-hand turn, went after them. Grim-faced and in complete control of himself once more, de la Mazière watched as the Yak pilot seemed to play with the panic-stricken racing civilians, waltzing from port to starboard, firing short bursts of tracer, stitching the snow at their heels with bullets, making the civilians break to left and right in their frantic efforts to save themselves from this flying monster.

De la Mazière's eyes narrowed. That would be the first one, he told himself. That sadistic bastard, still toying with the fleeing civilians, not realising that death was on his tail, would be the first one.

The trees and fields zipped past in a white blur. The Stuka hurtled through a black mushroom of ascending smoke from one of the burning carts. The tips of the pines almost seemed to be brushing the Stuka's wings as de la Mazière closed with the unsuspecting Yak. In the excitement of his cruel little game with the civilians, the Russian had still not looked in his rearview mirror. A hard gust of sudden wind buffeted the Stuka and threatened to throw it off course. De la Mazière grappled with the joystick, his shoulder muscles threatening to burst through the thin fabric of his black jacket. He gasped with the effort, body suddenly lathered in hot sweat. But he kept on course, teeth gritted with the strain.

Two hundred metres ahead of him, the Yak pilot tired suddenly of his game. He fell almost to the ground, cannon chattering crazily. Like a flight of angry hornets the 20mm shells went zipping towards the terrified civilians. At that range, the Russian could not miss. The shells slammed into the civilians, ripping them apart, flinging bits and pieces of flesh across the snow, dyeing it a mottled scarlet.

De la Mazière waited no longer. As the two other Yaks, now having spotted him, dived to the attack, he pressed his firing button. Savouring the sensation as one might enjoy caressing a

woman's naked body, he ran the tracer bullets the length of the Yak's fuselage, taking malicious pleasure at the sight of its fabric ripping and splinters of silver-gleaming metal falling away as the panicking pilot fought to keep his dying plane in the air. 'Now it's your turn, you Popov pig!' he
hissed, ignoring Hannemann's warning shouts. 'How does it feel to be at the other end of the iron, bastard?'

Abruptly the pilot lost control altogether. The Yak hit the snow. Its propeller bent backwards; its nose crumpled like a banana skin. It skidded along, trailing a wake of billowing snow behind it. Not for long. Next moment it burst into bright red flame, tinged with black. Its fuel tank had exploded.

Slugs ripped the length of the Stuka. Suddenly de la Mazière's nostrils were assailed by the stink of burning rubber and he felt a blast of icy cold air rushing in through the punctured fabric. Behind him Hannemann's machine gun began hammering away, the stench of burned cordite mixing with that of the rubber. He flung a quick glance into the rearview mirror. Both Yaks were on his tail, attacking him from port and starboard, brazen angry lights running the length of their wings as they hosed the long Stuka with fire.

He peered down at the ground. Beyond the blazing Yak, there was a steep rocky hillside split in two by a narrow gorge. Was it wide enough for him to fly through? Perhaps he could shake them off in there? Soviet pilot training was notoriously bad. With luck they'd either crash or be too afraid to follow him. He made a snap decision.

'Keep the buggers off my back, Hannemann!' he yelled exuberantly, feeling the heady thrill of close combat again as the adrenaline pumped into his blood-stream. He barrelled forward all-out, Hannemann firing furiously to left and right as the Yaks came in for the kill, already noting the thick white smoke beginning to pour from the Stuka's engine.

Desperately, weaving to left and right, willing the plane to make it into the gorge, ears expectant, waiting for the first throaty grunt that would indicate the engine was failing, de la Mazière flew on — barely conscious that his extreme tension was triggering reflexes so swift and immediate that he seemed to be flying better than he had ever done before, coming ever closer to the tight rocky entrance of the gorge.

'You're going to do it!' the urgent little voice within him yelled in triumph. 'You're going to do it, Detlev!'

But that wasn't to be.

Startlingly the cockpit was lit up a bright, evil, glowing red by the explosion of an incendiary bullet. De la Mazière registered a searing pain at the back of his neck. Suddenly everything happened fast. The fields vanished. On both sides there were stunted, snow-heavy pines rushing by at a tremendous rate. White liquid snow squirted the length of the windscreen and cut off his vision. Somehow he managed to drag up the Stuka's nose for a moment. 'Hannemann, we're getting out!' he shrieked. 'Belt off — canopy open!'

The cockpit cover flew away. There was the awesome impact of the wall of icy air. It felt as if he had been punched in the face by a gigantic fist. It forced his mouth open, wrenched his hands off the controls. The world spun crazily. Suddenly the bright white earth was above him. He felt himself falling. Desperately he prayed that the gorge would offer enough height for the chute to open. Hannemann went hurtling past him, head tucked into his knees, whirling round and round like a human cannonball, a piece of white paper or something fluttering from his back pocket. He vanished into that mad, whirling, upside-down world.

The earth was looming up to meet him. He was falling into a great hole. Below, in the white gloom, he could just make out what appeared to be a frozen-over stream. Suddenly there was a huge explosion. Bits of broken ice and a jet of muddy water erupted towards him. A second, more muffled explosion and a hiss of steam. The Stuka had crashed into the stream. He was still falling, falling, falling… A line of tall pines ran the length of the rock wall beneath him, like spike-helmeted Prussian guardsmen. In a minute they'd rip his body to pieces. He tensed, waiting for the impact, trying to lift his hands to protect his eyes, but failing; the air pressure was too great.

The chute opened with a tremendous crack. The straps tightened brutally around his body and threatened to tear his thigh bones out of their sockets. He howled with agony, his eyes flooding with tears. The trees were still rushing up to meet him, but he was not falling so fast as before. He prepared for the shock of the landing, his body oscillating violently to and fro. He slammed into something. Blood spurted into his boot. Another tremendous bang. Red stars exploded in front of his eyes. Madly he fought off unconsciousness. He was still dropping, his nostrils abruptly assailed by the sharp familiar smell of pine resin. A branch or something gave him a hideous smack across the forehead and he blacked out, suspended helplessly from the tree into which he had fallen.

He opened his eyes. Everything seemed to be wreathed in a green haze. He continued to hang there, numb with shock. His sense of balance had been shot to hell. He had the sensation he was still falling, spinning round and round at a dizzy pace. He shook his head and things slipped back into focus, as a wave of pain swept through his body. It felt as if his arms and legs had been torn off.

Someone was coming through the trees. Suddenly his pain was forgotten. Who could it be in this remote valley? He had to be kilometres away from the nearest German unit. Then his sudden tension vanished. Of course, it had to be Hannemann; he must have landed nearby.

He opened his mouth and licked his cracked parched lips. 'Sergeant Hannemann!' he called. 'Over here, Hannemann!... I'm caught up in some damned tree... Hanne —'

The cry died on his lips. A woman was standing there staring up at him. She wore a padded jacket and man's trousers, tucked into jackboots, but the face — broad, high-cheeked and Slavic beneath a fur hat — was pretty enough. But at that moment it was not the woman's pretty face that de la Mazière was looking at. It was the round-barrelled tommy-gun cradled to the woman's bosom like a precious child.

For what seemed an eternity the two of them froze thus, staring at each other, no sound breaking the heavy silence save that of the wind sighing in the pines.

Slowly, very slowly, the woman raised her tommy-gun and pointed it at the officer suspended from the tree above her head, closing one eye as she started to take aim...

CHAPTER 4

With a flick of his riding crop, von Nagy indicated to his servant that he wished to dismount. Immediately the soldier tumbled from his own horse and held up his clasped hands. Von Nagy placed one elegant booted foot in the handhold and allowed himself to be lowered into the snow. Tossing back his ankle-length, fur-lined cloak, he waited while his servant arranged the folds at the back, then strode off through the snow to the farmhouse Corps Commander's HQ.

Standing at the steamed-up window, General von Prittwitz smiled wryly. 'By God, Heinz,' he said to his aide, 'that's the way my great-grandfather must have treated his serfs! The Hungarians are a long-suffering people, it seems.'

Captain Heinz Linge nodded. 'Let us hope, General, that they continue to remain long-suffering — for the sake of XXX Corps.'

Von Prittwitz's smile vanished. He stared beyond von Nagy's approaching figure to the high snow-capped mountains to the west. They were the next obstacle in the Corps' retreat, and it would be von Nagy's task to find some pass in them through which he could send his soldiers and the poor civilians. 'I agree, Heinz, I agree. We desperately need that Hungarian cavalry for what is soon to come.' He raised his voice. 'See if we have any of that cognac left for His Excellency — and put out a couple of my personal cigars. We've got to spoil him this morning.'

A moment later von Nagy was ushered into the farm kitchen, which served as the XXX Corps' operations room, while outside the staff began to load up the essentials onto the remaining trucks and the little Polish *panje* wagons. By midday von Prittwitz wanted to be on his way westwards once more.

Von Prittwitz exchanged a few pleasantries with the Hungarian, offering him a cognac, which he accepted, and a cigar, which he declined; then he got straight down to business.

'Your Excellency,' he said, using the flowery formality that he knew the Hungarians loved, 'tomorrow my Corps will begin moving into the high mountains up there...' He indicated the snow-capped peaks through the window. 'I imagine that will reduce the enemy pressure on us because of the poor road system in the area. At all events, it will certainly slow down those damned T-34s of theirs.'

Von Nagy nodded his understanding, but made no comment. As always he was playing the game with his cards held close to his bemedalled chest.

'That is the positive side of the move into the mountains, Your Excellency. The negative aspect is this: unless we can find a suitable pass, both my infantry and the civilians will effectively be trapped; they are in no shape to tackle the mountains themselves. In that case XXX Corps might as well surrender to the Ivans now and have it done with.' That one blue eye of his stared at von Nagy, but there was no sign of defeat in his wizened old face in spite of his words. 'You understand, Your Excellency?'

'The passes in question,' the Hungarian General answered without hesitation, as if he had already been giving thought to the matter, 'are —' he stalked over to the map on the wall, his spurs jingling — 'from north-west to south-east. The Jablunkov Pass *here*, the Ruzomberok Pass *here*, and the Kezmarok Pass *here*.'

Von Prittwitz tensed suddenly. The last pass, Kezmarok Pass, was the closest to von Nagy's home country, Hungary.

Would he choose that one? And if so, would this indicate that the Hungarian Cavalry Division were preparing to defect to their own country? This was something that von Prittwitz had been fearing ever since the retreat had started.

Von Nagy took his time, staring hard at the map as if he were trying to find something that did not exist.

Outside, a coarse-voiced NCO was crying, 'Now come on, you asparagus Tarzans, heave them up! Put some back into it! Holy strawsack, some of you piss-pansies give me a headache right down to my arse!'

Finally von Nagy announced his decision. 'The Ruzomberok Pass. In the High Tatras.'

Von Prittwitz breathed an inner sigh of relief. The Hungarians weren't going to leave him in the lurch — not yet at least. 'I agree with your choice,' he said. 'It presents fewer defence problems tactically, although the terrain in the High Tatra Mountains at this time of the year will be pretty harsh. The question now is the best route through the pass…' He turned his one eye directly on the Magyar's craggy face. 'Will you find it for me, Your Excellency?' he asked simply.

Again von Nagy did not answer von Prittwitz's question directly. Instead he said, 'There is another problem you know nothing about, General.'

'There is?'

'The Slovaks.' Suddenly the Hungarian's face was animated by anger. 'Those damned peasant Slovaks! We should have wiped out the whole treacherous peasant bunch of them while we still had the opportunity!' His cheeks flushed red and his dark eyes blazed with rage. '*Slavic pigs*!' For a moment von Prittwitz thought he might have a stroke, he was so worked up.

'What exactly has happened, Your Excellency?'

Von Nagy controlled himself with difficulty. 'I have received information that the two infantry divisions of our so-called Slovakian "ally" stationed in Eastern Slovakia might go over to the partisans, now that the Red Army is advancing on their country. As usual, the rats are leaving the sinking ship!'

It was not until much later that von Prittwitz would ask himself how von Nagy had received this information. All he said now was: 'It is then a matter of getting to the pass and through the mountains before that eventuality occurs.'

'Agreed, General.'

'You will do it for me — find the best way through?' von Prittwitz asked urgently.

'Yes — on one condition,' von Nagy answered.

'And that is?'

Once again the Hungarian did not answer the Corps Commander directly. He said instead, 'In the last forty-eight hours, General, my division has suffered serious casualties. Both my men at point and those at the rear-guard have taken bad losses.'

'I know, and I sympathise with you on the loss of your brave fellows.'

Von Nagy ignored the comment. 'When the news of such casualties reaches Budapest, there will be trouble. The political climate is very uncertain in my poor country now. Losses unsettle the people and make the demands for peace with the Bolsheviks even more urgent. General von Prittwitz, I cannot afford to suffer any more such losses.'

Suddenly the old soldier could see von Nagy's inner conflict revealed on his face. It was the conflict between doing his duty as a loyal soldier to his German ally and placating public opinion back in his own country. Abruptly von Prittwitz felt very sorry for the Hungarian. But all he said was: 'So…?'

Von Nagy did not hesitate this time. 'I request all possible air cover for the reconnaissance of the Ruzomberok Pass. Herr General, I need that flying artillery of yours — desperately!'

Von Prittwitz paused thoughtfully, examining the naked emotion on the Magyar's craggy features. The enemy was pressing in the whole perimeter of his rolling goose-egg. The SS Stuka Wing was needed virtually everywhere. Yet he could not refuse the Hungarian. 'You have it, Your Excellency. You will have what is left of the 1st SS Stuka Wing for the whole duration of the operation in the Ruzomberok Pass.'

Von Nagy heaved an audible sigh of relief. 'Thank you, General. You do not know what a load that takes off my mind.' He took his elegant cap and placed it on his pomaded curls. He clicked his heels together and touched the peak of his cap. 'General, I bid you goodbye. *Auf Wiedersehen.*'

'*Auf Wiedersehen,*' von Prittwitz echoed, amused as ever at the formality of these Hungarian soldiers. He waited until the cavalry officer and his orderly had begun to canter away through the snow, ignoring the German headquarters soldiers who lined their path standing rigidly to attention. Then he called, 'Heinz!'

'Sir?' His aide popped his head round the rough wooden kitchen door, as if he had been standing there all the time — which he had. 'You want me to call the 1st SS?'

Von Prittwitz chuckled. 'Why you young rogue, you were listen—' He stopped short when he saw that Heinz had his automatic clutched in his right hand. And behind him were several steel-helmeted 'chain dogs', hard-faced and grim, hugging machine pistols to their burly chests. 'Why the cannon and the chain dogs?' he rasped.

Heinz put his pistol away and dismissed the MPs with a nod. 'Just taking precautions, sir.'

'Against what, pray?'

'There's a whole regiment of Hungarian cavalry up there on the ridge, sir. One of our couriers spotted them. In other words, von Nagy did not come alone, sir — and I wasn't taking any chances that something might happen to you. Hence the chain dogs.'

Von Prittwitz frowned in bewilderment. 'I don't understand…'

'I don't either, sir, really,' Heinz confessed. 'But why bring that kind of escort with you — over five hundred heavily armed men?' Now it was the handsome young officer's turn to frown. 'I don't know how to put it, sir … but somehow I think if things had not gone right for General von Nagy in this room, those Hungarian cavalrymen of his might well have been taking over this headquarters by now.'

The old Corps Commander glared at him, that one blue eye glittering. 'You don't know what you're saying, Heinz.'

The aide flushed a bright red. 'Sir, I know the Hungarians are our allies, and so far von Nagy's cavalry have proved tremendously loyal, taking the same knocks as our own poor stubble-hoppers, but…' He struggled to formulate his thoughts in words. 'But they were definitely up to something today. I'm sure they were. At least…' His words tailed away lamely.

'Have the cavalry gone now?'

'Yessir. As soon as von Nagy left your HQ, sir, they started moving out. I had an observer up there on the roof of the barn, watching them through his glasses.'

Von Prittwitz sucked his bottom teeth, trying to puzzle out the mystery. Heinz was right, of course. Why bring an escort of such strength and then hide them? Yet von Nagy had been co-operative enough; and he had seen enough of the Hungarian in these last terrible months on the Eastern Front to know that he was not lying when he promised his support for the operations in the Ruzomberok Pass. Finally he gave up and shrugged angrily. Outside, the first *panje* wagons laden with equipment were beginning to move out, the little Polish ponies pulling the carts urged on by their drivers. The headquarters was leaving. He didn't have much time left. 'All right, let's forget it, Heinz. Von Nagy is with us, of that I am sure… At the double, contact the HQ of the 1st Stuka. I wish to speak to Colonel de la Mazière at once. Top priority — it is of the utmost importance.'

'Sir.' Heinz closed the door behind him and hurried away.

The old Corps Commander went to the window and stood there for several minutes, absently rubbing his cheek with his gloved artificial hand while he stared at the high peaks of the Tatra Mountains, wondering what exactly was going on up there…

CHAPTER 5

A thin mist writhed eerily over the surface of the frozen river, its edges tinged a bright silver by the half-moon. Now the night was silent save for the mysterious rustle of wind in the spectral pines and, far away, the soft boom of Russian artillery. Sergeant Hannemann, frozen and hungry, could almost have thought he was all alone in this remote hidden valley, but he knew that was not true. They were down there somewhere, further along the frozen river, and they had de la Mazière with them.

Hannemann had been watching when they took him. The gigantic woman in a padded jacket and trousers had cursed and hurriedly knocked up the first woman's tommy-gun in the very instant that she fired at de la Mazière hanging there helplessly from the tree by his shroud lines. Hannemann had been about to tackle the two of them, although he was armed only with a pistol and a single hand grenade. Fortunately he had not done so. For just then half a hundred of them — all women, all heavily armed — had emerged from among the pines and had set about the task of getting de la Mazière down from the tree under the direction of the female giant.

Ten minutes later they had been on their way, dragging de la Mazière behind them, hands tied behind his back and a long halter around his neck — like some damned animal, an enraged Hannemann had told himself, fists clenched in frustration, being led off to the knacker's yard.

All that afternoon he had followed them, his stomach rumbling ever more insistently, though he'd managed to quench his thirst with handfuls of snow. And all that afternoon his fury had mounted at the way the women partisans treated the Old Man. More than once, when he had not stumbled to his feet quickly enough after a rest-break, the female giant with black cropped hair had slashed at de la Mazière's face with a strange-looking knout. By the time they had reached the straggling collection of *isbas* where they were evidently making camp for the night, de la Mazière's face was swollen and puffed up, both eyes narrowed to slits, his left cheek one livid bruise.

When the big woman began to post sentries for the night, Hannemann had hastily backed off from the straw-roofed peasant huts and taken cover in the firs to think out his position. By now he had guessed with whom he was dealing: Red Rosa and the 'Sisters of Soviet Blood', as they were called officially in both the Soviet and German Press, the feared female partisan group composed of women who had lost a relative in battle against the Germans, all of whom had sworn an oath to kill half a hundred 'Fritzes' before they fell in battle.

All that winter, rumours had circulated among the half-scared soldiers of the XXX Corps about the daring exploits of Red Rosa and her Sisters of Soviet Blood: how, disguised as peasant women, they had wormed their way into a German HQ and abducted a full general; how they had set up what seemed to be a mobile brothel in the 10th Division's rear, and then emasculated some twenty unfortunate stubble-hoppers before they had been discovered and had fled for their lives; how they had booby-trapped the bed of the local County Party Leader and blown him and his Polack mistress to kingdom-come while they were engaged in a little mattress polka. 'Fall into the hands o' them Popov bitches, comrades,' the awed and frightened soldiers had whispered to each other in their freezing trenches at night, 'and they'll slice off yer dong as soon as look at yer — and that's only fer starters! Did yer hear where they stuck the bayonet o' that poor swine they captured the other day?...'

Now de la Mazière had fallen into their hands and Hannemann, crawling cautiously through the mist around the little hutted camp at this moment, knew with the
certainty of a vision that the CO wouldn't survive the new day. They'd torture what information they wanted out of him. Red Rosa, with her bull's pizzle — for now Hannemann knew that was what her knout was — was an expert in torture. And then they'd kill him. Somehow or other Hannemann had to rescue the Old Man. But how? What could he do against fifty or more well-armed and ruthless females?

De la Mazière shifted his position the best he could, moaning softly as a knife-like pain stabbed into his side. He hoped the big woman hadn't broken his ribs with that monstrous bull's pizzle she affected. Suddenly he smiled in spite of the pain. What did it matter really? Hadn't she laid it on the line to him just before she had left?

Surrounded by her Sisters, raw-boned, heavy-bosomed peasant women mostly in their thirties, she had growled, 'Fritz, you talk in the morning, then you die.' Then she had taken the black cigar from between her thick red sensuous lips and quite deliberately pressed it against his naked arm. '*Ponemayo* ... understand? Talk — or else!' She had made a cutting motion towards his belly with the cigar and the other women had laughed gruffly. With that, one big arm draped protectively around the neck of one of the prettier women, she had swaggered out, leaving de la Mazière in no doubt about her intentions. If he talked, he would die a clean death. If he didn't… He shuddered and did not dare think that particular thought to its awful end.

Now the camp lay quiet in sleep, no sound disturbing the night save for the soft crunch of the female sentry's boots on the frozen snow. Red Rosa ran her regiment of Sisters as a regular military formation; there was nothing of the soft silly female about her and her followers.

De la Mazière propped himself up on his elbows, wincing as the rope bit cruelly into the soft flesh of his wrists tied behind his back, and considered his position. In the old days, the loss of one of their Stukas would have prompted the Wing to launch a full-scale search. Other pilots would have risked their necks to land next to the wreckage and attempt to find out what had happened to the Colonel and his Sergeant. But not now. The majority of the pilots were greenbeaks, scared of making independent decisions; the rest, the veterans, were old, cynical, wily, intent on saving their own precious skins now that they knew the war was virtually lost in the East. Perhaps one or two might have tried: the 'retreads', as they called themselves, who had been with the 1st SS in the old days; but not with Baron Karst now in charge of the Wing. Karst, his second-in-command, hated de la Mazière with a passion. He would have found a dozen good military reasons for not allowing out search planes. No, de la Mazière told himself, as he lay there in that remote valley preparing himself for certain death on the morrow, the Karsts had taken over in Germany; there was no hope from that quarter. By this time tomorrow he would be dead, his mutilated corpse thrown into some snow-filled hollow to wait there for the wolves.

Racked up like corpses in the ledges lining the warm sides of the huge stove that reached to the blackened ceiling, they snored, the pilots of the 1st SS Stuka Wing ... all save Baron Karst. Tired as he was, he simply could not sleep.

At last, after five long years, Karst was in command of the 1st SS Stuka. Lying there, hands tucked beneath his head, listening to the snoring all around him, the crackle of logs in the fire, the wind howling in the eaves of the peasant's hut, forgetting the fleas with which they were all infected and the gnawing pangs of hunger in the base of his stomach, he allowed himself a cold smile.

His fellows, members of the 'old aristocracy', had always despised him in spite of the title he bore. They knew that his great-grandfather had been ennobled by the King of Prussia for his industry and his ability on the shopfloor of the steel works that he had built up in the middle of the nineteenth century. The Karsts had not simply inherited a title; they had *worked* for it. But the others, de la Mazière and the like, had never wanted to understand that. Karst's ancestor belonged to the 'trade', as they put it in their supercilious fashion, forgetting that their forefathers had been nothing better than robber barons who had made their fortunes by theft and blackmail.

But Karst had outlived them all. *He* was the new commander of the 1st SS Stuka Wing, once feted in the Poison Dwarfs Press as the 'élite of the élite'. 'The Black Guards with Wings' was how that little club-footed Dr Goebbels had phrased it in the great days of 1940, when the magic name of 'Stuka' had been on everybody's tongue.

'Colonel Baron Karst, Commander the 1st SS Stuka Wing...' He savoured the title lovingly, telling himself he had done it — at last.

In the glowing darkness he frowned. But what could he do with that title out here in this God-forsaken place? He had no confidence in von Prittwitz's plan to roll the 'goose-egg' to safety in Slovakia. Sooner or later the Russians would swamp them — and what would happen to him and his Wing then? They would be wiped out. They would be forgotten, like those stupid idiots at Stalingrad last year. There was no more glory to be won in Russia. Somehow or other he had to get himself and his men to the West and safety while there was still time. But how? *How*, damn it, *how*?

Karst let his mind wander, trying to find a solution. He knew that his was an independent command; he was responsible solely to Reichsführer SS Himmler — and, in a way, to that fat clown Göring. He could go, if he wished, and von Prittwitz could not do a thing about it. But somehow the news that he had abandoned the front would get back to Berlin, and his reputation would be tarnished. No, he told himself as he lay there on that narrow hot shelf, that was not the way.

Time passed with leaden feet as he wrestled with his problem. And then at last he had it. He had found his solution. Of course, he told himself, such things happen all the time! No one would be able to criticise him. Commanders often had to abort missions under such circumstances… Suddenly Karst gave a heart-felt sigh of relief. Five minutes later he was snoring as heartily as the rest.

Thus it was that he did not hear the soft tread of someone stealing into the fetid hot room, full of the smell of black tobacco, stale cabbage and human sweat. Nor did he hear the whispering as Slack-Arse Schmidt awoke the oldest 'retread' of them all, Major von Kramm, known as 'Pegleg'.

'Sir, it's two hours to dawn… The plane's gassed up, engine warm, ready to go.'

Von Kramm took the flatman that Slack-Arse offered and swallowed a satisfying slug of firewater. 'All right, Schmidt, ready to go,' he whispered. 'Where's my shitting leg now…?'

Slack-Arse breathed a sigh of relief as he handed the Major his awkward-looking artificial limb. Pegleg was going to go through with it, thank God!

Hannemann hesitated no longer. The freezing cold was creeping into his very bones. If he didn't act now, he would soon be unable to move. Hardly daring to breathe, heart thudding away as if it might burst at any moment, he crept out of the trees towards the lone woman sentry standing there in the mist, body fat and clumsy in her thick jacket, tommy-gun clutched to her bosom. For such a big man Hannemann moved exceedingly softly. One false move, he knew, and the whole damned camp would be alarmed — and that would be that.

Now he was ten metres or less from the sentry. Already he could smell her typical Russian odour, a mixture of black Makhorka tobacco, garlic, unwashed body and something else that was essentially feminine. Five metres. Still the woman stood there motionless as a statue. Suddenly it came to him that he would have to kill her. A woman. In cold blood. He stopped for an instant, shocked by that sudden realisation. He had never killed a woman before, not in all the years he had been in combat. *Kill a woman?* Women were for fucking, not killing!

Then he thought of de la Mazière and what these same women would do to him in the morning. His jaw hardened. He stepped forward. Abruptly it happened. The sentry turned. For one long, heart-thumping eternity they stared at each other, the murderer and his victim, her face surprisingly gentle and pretty in the cold silver light of the moon — and unafraid. She opened her mouth to shout.

Hannemann dived forward. The woman side-stepped. Desperately Hannemann flung out his right hand as he hit the snow. He was lucky. His huge paw caught the woman and bowled her off her feet. She fell face forward, her cry of alarm muffled by the snow. Hannemann threw himself on top of her. She reacted instantly. Her gloved hand sought and found his genitals, and twisted them. Hannemann writhed frantically, biting his lip to prevent himself from crying out. Blindly he thrust out a hand to seize the woman's throat. She sank her teeth into the soft flesh of his thumb, still grasping his genitals. He twisted and turned, trying to break that vice-like grip, sweat streaming down his wildly contorted face.

Sobbing for breath, feeling the black veil of unconsciousness threatening to overcome him at any moment as her cruel fingers bit deeper and deeper into his genitals, Hannemann smashed his left fist into her face. Once, twice, three times. Something burst. He felt the knuckles of his hand wet with blood. Still she held on.

'Let go, you cow! Let go!' he gasped as the electric agony seared his loins. Any minute now he'd black out. He hit her again with all his remaining strength. Her grip seemed to weaken. Once more he smashed his fist into her face. She was letting go. Blood was spurting from her broken, pulped nostrils now. She was breathing in short, harsh, hectic gasps, as if she were drugged. He hit her once more. Still she struggled, but her grip on his testicles was getting weaker. He heaved his lower body. The pain was murderous. He dug his teeth into his bottom lip to stifle his scream. His mouth was flooded with copper-tasting hot blood. Suddenly — blessedly — the agony was gone from his loins. He could have lain there and sobbed with relief. But he knew there was no time for that.

He squirmed round and above the woman. Her face was battered into an almost unrecognisable pulp, eyes narrowed to slits, cheeks already pulling up and patched by scarlet bleeding bruises. Her teeth glittered like white ivory through the mess of cherry-red blood. For one long moment he hesitated, staring down at her ... but she glared back at him, defiant to the very last, knowing that he would show no mercy now, knowing that she was going to die.

In that moment, poised thus, Hannemann knew that what he was going to do now would brand him indelibly for the rest of his life. If he survived the war, it would be with him for ever, to haunt him all his days, never to be forgotten, carried with him always like the mark of Cain.

Suddenly the woman pursed those terrible cherry-red lips and spat a gob of bright red blood right into his face. It released the spring. With the blood dripping down his cheek, he thrust those big killing hands around her neck and applied the pressure.

She writhed and wriggled, eyes popping out, head thrown back, spine arched and pelvis thrust forward, breath coming in quick strangled gasps as if she were in the throes of sexual passion.

He exerted all his strength. Sweat streamed down his face and mingled with the blood. Now he too was gasping, like some ancient asthmatic. His heart thundered. His nerves jangled. 'Die, you bitch!' he croaked. 'For God's sake ... *die*!'

She thrust up her lower body. He felt the heat of her stomach pressed into his as she twisted and turned in the snow, trying in vain to escape his murderous grip. Her soft belly pressed against him, harder and harder. Her warmth seared into his loins. He could not help himself. 'No,' he pleaded with his body, 'please … no!'

But there was no stopping it. Perversely, horrifyingly, he felt that old familiar stirring. It couldn't be! But it was… Even as he was strangling her Hannemann felt a burning passion for this unknown Russian woman who had tried to kill him. It was unbelievable. 'NO!' he cried aloud. But his body would not obey him.

With one last awesome surge of strength, she thrust the length of her body against his. It was unbearable. He could feel everything: plump breasts, soft stomach, hard circle of bone around the Mount of Venus — he even imagined that he could feel the hard curls of that secret hair. His passion flamed. At that moment he could have pressed his lips against hers, broken and bloodied as they were, and smothered them with wild abandoned kisses.

Suddenly she went limp. Dead, in the very instant that his lower body was racked by an almost impossible ecstasy. His loins flooded joyously. All strength fled from him. He collapsed weakly on the dead body, murderer and victim clasped in a lethal embrace, and he sobbed aloud with passion and remorse.

CHAPTER 6

Dawn came reluctantly. To the east, the sun was poised a weak watery yellow on the horizon, as if not daring to rise any further and illuminate this stark, war-torn world.

The two of them swayed to a halt, gasping broken-lunged for breath, staggering to the cover of the snow-heavy trees like two drunks, eyes blank and seeing only the support of the nearest trunk.

Thirty minutes after that terrible murder, Hannemann had found and freed de la Mazière. They had escaped completely unnoticed, but now they both knew that the hue-and-cry had been raised. Twice they had heard faint cries of anger and alarm further down the valley; and once there had been the sharp startling chatter of a Soviet tommy-gun. Obviously whoever had fired it had been signalling to the rest of the Sisters. No doubt their footprints had been found in the fresh sprinkling of new snow that had fallen just before dawn. Now they were hunted men, lost in this snowy wilderness, so remote from their own troops that they could no longer hear the rumble of the permanent barrage.

Hannemann pulled himself together and wiped the end of his dripping red nose. 'What do you think, sir?' he panted, staring back the way they would come. The snow was beginning to sparkle in crystalline beauty in the first rays of the sun. But there was no sign of their pursuers.

'Not much,' de la Mazière gasped, moving his head to ease the stiffness caused by the wound on his neck. 'We're heading in the general direction of our troops — they stole my compass, though, so I can't say exactly where we are. God knows just how far we've got to go before we meet up with our own men.' He frowned and sucked his teeth despondently.

Hannemann put a bold face on it. 'Well, sir, we're still alive — and kicking. We'll outrun those Popov pussies yet. You never know, sir, we might meet that civilian trek that the Yaks shot up.' He forced an encouraging smile, though he had never felt less like smiling in all his life.

'Elephants might fly,' de la Mazière said miserably. 'All right, you big rogue, let's make tracks again.' Stiffly he levered himself up from the stump on which they'd been sitting and staggered out into the open once more.

Wearily Hannemann did the same, forcing his tired legs forward as he stumbled after de la Mazière, placing his feet in the imprints the Colonel had left behind him. It was the old trick of keeping going when one was absolutely, totally exhausted; and no one, Hannemann told himself, knew better how to keep going at the end of one's tether than the aristocrats of the SS.

One hour later, the Sisters caught up with them. They were beginning to ascend a steep rocky slope, stumbling and slipping on the new snow, grabbing at handholds in the rocks or clumps of frozen gorse to haul themselves up, when that first startling command came from below.

'*Stoi!*'

'It's them!' de la Mazière gasped, chest heaving madly.

There was the sharp crack of a single rifle shot, like a dry twig snapping underfoot. Almost immediately a tommy-gun opened up with a furious chatter and a line of hissing, steaming holes was stitched across the snowy cliff-face just ahead of them.

Hannemann flung a look over his shoulder. A bunch of the Sisters in their familiar bulky jackets had burst out of the firs to the right and were kneeling now in the snow, firing at them.

The sight of their pursuers lent new strength to their weary limbs. As slugs began to howl and whine off the rocks all about them, the two men scrambled higher up the cliff. More of the Sisters were hurrying out of the trees, slinging their weapons and beginning the ascent after them, urged on by Red Rosa, slapping her monstrous bull-pizzle against the side of her jackboot impatiently.

Now they were climbing for all they were worth, eyes fixed on the top of the rock face, as if Salvation itself lay there waiting for them. '*Los, los*!' de la Mazière gasped urgently. 'Keep going, Hannemann! You can't give up now... *Los*!'

Hannemann could not answer; he had not the breath to do so. He was starting to lag behind, unable to keep up with the Colonel, who had been a skilled rock-climber before the war and who was now employing all the old tricks to lessen the strain of the ascent. Below him he could hear the excited cries of the women as they closed on him, urged on by bellows from Red Rosa.

'*Davai, davai*!... Kill the swine!... KILL!'

De la Mazière swung himself over the top and lay full length there for a few seconds, everything swimming before his eyes, his heart thumping madly as if it might burst out of his ribcage. He shook his head. The scene swung into focus once more. The first of the women — a brute of a wench with a hard dark gypsy face — was only a matter of metres behind the straining, crimson-faced Hannemann. Already she had stopped and was balancing herself on a protruding boulder, ripping off her tommy-gun. Her intention was obvious. In a moment she would rip Hannemann's back apart with a burst.

Frantically de la Mazière scrabbled in the snow. He had it. A fist-sized rock. He balanced it in his frozen hand, then flung it with all his strength. His aim was true. The rock hit the woman squarely in the chest. She teetered backwards, fighting desperately to keep her balance, tommy-gun falling from her hands, flailing her arms in her efforts to stave off the inevitable. Suddenly with a terrible shriek she went over, falling head first to her death on the rocks at the foot of the cliff-face. A moment later de la Mazière had grabbed Hannemann's hand and was hauling him up over the top of the cliff.

'Thanks … thanks,' Hannemann gasped, lungs wheezing like cracked leathern bellows.

'Forget it, you big rogue. Come on. But give me that auto —'

'Use the grenade, sir,' Hannemann interrupted. 'More effective when they're bunched like that. We'll save the pistol in case…' He didn't finish the sentence, but de la Mazière, busy with the stick grenade, knew what he meant. They'd save those last bullets for themselves; suicide was preferable to falling into the hands of the Sisters once more.

De la Mazière pulled out the china pin, raised the grenade above his head and tossed it neatly into a group of six of the women panting their way to the top. It exploded in a vicious ball of yellow-red flame, right in their midst. The air was rent by piercing screams of agony as the women went reeling back, their clothes shredded and blackened, stained here and there by sudden scarlet, to hurtle over the cliffside and strike the ground below with an awesome impact, and lie still.

That stopped the rush — for a while. But even as a weary de la Mazière seized Hannemann's arm and forced him to move on across the limitless snow plain that stretched right to the horizon before them, he knew it would not be long before Red Rosa and her sadistic Sisters would be after them again.

'All of us old Stuka pilots,' Pegleg was saying between sips from his flatman, 'end up in the funny farm eventually. One day you can't take any more of it — the dive-bombing, the fact you're flying a crate that's years out of date, the enemy fighters — and you start pulling your clothes off, or pissing on the mess table, or going off in a corner with your finger in your mouth, face to the wall, as if you were the school dunce.' He took another sip of fiery vodka and belched delicately. 'And then the friendly fellows in the white coats come to take you away in the rubber car. It's the funny farm for you, pal.'

Half listening, an anxious Slack-Arse peered to left and right, searching for any sign of the two missing men. They had spotted the site where the Stuka had gone down half an hour before, an area of charred melted snow with the tell-tale scattering of shattered metal. Since then they had been flying in ever-widening circles over the snowy hills and plains, searching for the Old Man and Hanneman.

'Yes,' Pegleg went on, 'the funny farm is where all your old heads of the Stuka squadrons end up these days, Sergeant. A few of them manage to come back to the fighting squadrons as retreads. And they have to be cuckoo to do so.' He laughed bitterly. 'Nobody who's got all his cups in his cupboard — except for our greenbeaks, but they're still wet behind the spoons — would volunteer to fly the Stuka any more. You might as well volunteer to put your turnip under the tracks of a moving Tiger tank!' Again he gave that bitter laugh and took another sip of vodka. 'Stukas — I've shit 'em!' he added vehemently.

Slack-Arse forgot his missing CO and running-mate for a moment. 'But you should have seen them back in Spain — Barcelona, Alicante, Valencia. We put the fear of death into the Reds then, sir, when we came falling out of the sky, sirens howling, going all out. It was the same in France in nineteen-forty, even in Russia back at the beginning...' He sighed fondly. 'Those were the days, sir!'

'History, Sergeant,' Pegleg said cynically, 'ancient shitting history! Nowadays you take your life into your hands the very moment you put your foot inside a Stuka.'

'Well, why do they keep on making 'em, sir?' Slack-Arse asked, genuinely puzzled. 'They could make a more up-to-date plane if they wanted, couldn't they?'

'They, my dear Sergeant Schmidt,' Pegleg answered, 'are crazy. Crazy as loons up there at the top, all of them. One day the friendly fellows in white coats will come for them, too, and take them off to the funny farm in the rubber car. I hope to live that long. Now, let's forget this ancient bird and concentrate our glassy orbits on the terrain.'

They flew on.

Now they were running for their lives. Somehow the Sisters had got into the wood in front of them. There was no mistaking those excited Russian cries and calls ahead of them. It was Red Rosa's female monsters all right. Blundering, stumbling, the two men fought their way back through the trees, the branches lashing their faces cruelly, ripping at their clothes, hindering their terrified progress, as their hunters came closer and closer.

De la Mazière pushed Hannemann into the lead, the NCO's pistol clutched in his own damp fist. He would take four of them with him before he shot Hannemann and himself, he told himself, as they stumbled on, gasping fervently for breath, their faces lathered in sweat, breath coming in great white clouds, jetting in hectic spurts from their distended nostrils.

The forest started to thin out. 'Keep going, Hannemann!' he urged. He paused momentarily and fired, his hand trembling violently. One of the grey shapes to his rear slammed to the ground without a sound. 'Keep going!'

Hannemann moaned. 'I've had a noseful, sir... Can't keep going ... much longer...'

'Course you can!' De la Mazière halted, legs without feeling, as if they were made of soft rubber. A burst of tommy-gun bullets ripped the trees to his front. A rain of green came tumbling down, alerting him to his danger. He fired. To his right, the Sister who had fired dropped her tommy-gun, fanning the air with her hands as if she were climbing the rungs of an invisible ladder, desperately trying to stay upright and alive. It wasn't to be. With a sad little sigh, like some old granny might make at the naughtiness of a beloved child, she sank gently to the snow and died.

They staggered on, trying to ignore the pain stabbing their tortured lungs, the burning cramps in their leg muscles, the almost overwhelming desire to just lie down in the snow and submit to the blessed oblivion, have it done with once and for all...

Suddenly Hannemann's feet went from underneath him. He sprawled full length, the last of his breath knocked from his lungs, face buried in the snow, great shoulders heaving violently as if he were sobbing broken-hearted.

De la Mazière skidded to a stop. The women were after them again. They were less than fifty metres away, shrieking in triumph, surging towards the fallen man in a rough, clumsy skirmish line. He dropped to one knee, his hand holding the automatic still shaking like an aspen leaf. The pistol's sights dissected the gigantic bulk of Red Rosa. He tried to calm his frantic breathing, telling himself that if he knocked her out the others might weaken. He took first pressure … second … desperately trying to steady his hand. He fired.

The pistol kicked upwards. His nostrils were assailed by the stink of burned cordite. The bullet dug up a little spurt of snow — metres in front of the big Russian woman. He had missed her. 'Shit!' he cursed and bent over Hannemann, heaving him across his shoulder like a sack of potatoes and stumbling a few yards towards a clearing in the trees. But his strength was ebbing fast. He stopped, lowering the big noncom against a rock.

Hannemann's blue lips moved, but no words came. He was looking at the pistol in the Colonel's hand.

De la Mazière shook his head. 'No,' he said, feeling the resolution drain from his body. '*No* — not yet.'

'Then what…' Hannemann managed to croak, 'what do we do?'

De la Mazière did not know. Slowly, infinitely slowly, he started to lower the pistol as he knelt there at Hannemann's side.

The Sisters rushed in for the kill…

'There they are!' Slack-Arse yelled, voice shrill and urgent over the intercom. 'At ten o'clock, sir — in that clearing!'

Pegleg almost dropped the precious flatman from his lap with surprise. 'Holy strawsack, you're right, Schmidt! It's the Old Man. I'd recognise that blond thatch anywhere.' He peered down at the semicircle of dark figures closing in on the two men crouched next to a rock. 'And it looks as if the Old Man has been caught with his hooter deep in the proverbial shit! Come on!'

He closed the throttle slowly. The aircraft started to drop. The ground rushed up to meet them. 'What are you going to do, sir?' Slack-Arse yelled in sudden alarm.

'That's our commanding officer down there, Sergeant. His charger's obviously been shot away from beneath him. Can't do less than offer him mine. Gonna land.' Pegleg burst out in a loud grinding laugh.

Slack-Arse, lapsed Catholic that he was, crossed himself swiftly. Now he knew what Pegleg meant about the 'friendly fellows in white overalls'. That clearing was surely too small to land a plane in; there were trees all around it, and rocks dotted everywhere. If this sort of thing went on much longer, he'd soon be a candidate for the 'funny farm' himself.

Down below, the Sisters had spotted what the lone Stuka was up to. They stopped their charge forward. Raising their tommy-guns, they commenced firing wildly as the Stuka came soaring in above the trees, the snow whisked upwards in a thick white swirling fog by its engine. Tracer zipped past the plane in red and white fury. Slack-Arse cursed. Awkwardly, teeth gritted against the pain of his wounded shoulder, he swung his machine gun round as far as it would go, and ripped off a wild, unaimed burst. It had the desired effect. The Sisters dashed for cover and the firing stopped abruptly.

'*Prima*!' Pegleg called joyously. 'For a peasant, you can really think! Haven't got your arse in your face like most of 'em have.'

'Plush tits!' Slack-Arse snorted.

Now Pegleg concentrated on the landing. 'Throttle back,' he commanded, speaking to himself like most pilots. 'Flaps down. Watch you don't overshoot. Hold her straight — for Chrissake, *hold her straight*!... Here we go!'

The Stuka hit the ground heavily, lurched as it hit a rock, and rolled forward, snow spurting up on both sides. The plane had landed — and it was directly between the two comrades and their pursuers.

Hastily Pegleg thrust back the canopy, gunning the engine as he did so. He was taking no chances now with the Popovs only metres away. 'Your coach awaits you, milord!' he yelled at de la Mazière over the top of the open cockpit.

'Shit in the wind, sir!' Slack-Arse screamed. 'Get yer turnip down, sir, or the Ivans'll knock it off in a half mo!' Pegleg was absolutely crazy; he didn't seem to know what fear meant.

Bullets were ripping the length of the plane in frustrated fury as the two fugitives dashed towards it on the other side, arms pumping, faces grim with determination, while Slack-Arse hosed the snow to the right with his machine gun, trying desperately to keep the Ivans at bay.

Suddenly Slack-Arse gasped. 'Great crap on the Christmas tree! They're *women*! Must be them Sisters of the Soviet Blood! Holy shit, sir!'

But Pegleg did not seem to hear. He was standing upright in the cockpit, grinning like a loon, totally unafraid, waving at the two men ploughing through the snow like a spectator at a horserace.

De la Mazière reached the plane first. He waited for Hannemann, his face lathered in sweat and ashen-grey. 'Come on,' he choked and, clasping his hands together, bent so that the NCO could use them as a step.

Slack-Arse stopped firing for a moment. 'Hot shit,' he muttered to himself as de la Mazière heaved the exhausted Sergeant aboard. 'Now I've seen everything. One of them aristocratic pisspots helping one of us peasants!' He squeezed to one side as Hannemann slumped down beside him, eyes closed, totally out.

A moment later de la Mazière was squeezing in beside Pegleg. The pilot slammed the canopy closed. 'Hold tight!' he cried, taking a hasty slug from his flatman as he opened the throttle with his other hand.

'Watch the snow, Pegleg!' de la Mazière cried in alarm.

'What went down has to come up, as the pavement pounder said,' Pegleg chortled, grinning all over his broad face.

The heavily laden Stuka began to roll slowly forward. Then suddenly it lurched to a stop, tyres skidding on the snow. Slack-Arse moaned and, with frantic fingers that felt as clumsy as thick sausages, began to feed a new belt of ammunition into the machine gun. Already the first of the Sisters were abandoning the cover of the trees and starting to rush across to the plane. If they didn't get off the ground in a moment, there would be all hell to pay.

Pegleg revved the engine even more, while beside him de la Mazière clenched his fists in desperation, willing the plane to move before it was too late.

'*Davai, davai*!' Red Rosa screamed at the women, leading the rush towards the plane and thrashing the air with her bull's pizzle. They were spreading out now, and firing as they floundered through the snow.

'Come on ... come on, you stinking bitch!' Slack-Arse cursed, still fumbling with the ammunition belt. The Sisters were only twenty metres away now. Slugs were riddling the fuselage. The tail was already shredded, holed everywhere. Another minute and they would be done for.

The Stuka slithered to the right. Now Pegleg's grin had vanished as he fought the controls, trying to keep the plane moving. The women were only ten metres away now. The slugs cut the air on all sides. In a moment it would all be over. They *had* to get off the ground…

Suddenly they were rolling. The tail lifted. Their speed was increasing. Amid a flurry of white, the plane trundled forward. A slug slammed against the side of the canopy, where it wasn't bullet-proof, and the women disappeared from view in a spider's web of gleaming splintered perspex. The plane rolled on. Sweating and red-faced, Pegleg pulled back the stick. Nothing happened.

At his side, cramped and anxious, de la Mazière cried out in despair: 'We're not going to make it!'

'Don't worry,' Pegleg growled through gritted teeth, 'the funny farm boys won't let you down…' He heaved at the stick again. The Stuka lifted — but only for a moment. Next instant it hit the ground again with a bone-jarring smack. Pegleg cursed under his breath. He tried again. This time it worked. They were airborne! The ground was fast receding below them; the women were left staring up at them in frustrated rage, becoming tiny black shapes and then disappearing altogether.

They had done it. They were getting away with it.

Behind the two happy officers, their sweat-lathered faces wreathed in huge smiles, babbling away like crazy schoolboys, Slack-Arse slumped over his gun, exhausted. Next to him an ashen-faced Hannemann slowly opened his eyes, as if he could hardly believe they were actually airborne. 'Holy strawsack — what a performance!' he croaked. Then: 'I think I've gone an' pissed in me boots, Slack-Arse…'

His old running-mate did not have the strength to reply.

The plane flew on.

CHAPTER 7

Papa Diercks, the white-haired senior crew chief — it was rumoured that he had once been crew chief to no less a person than von Richthofen himself — flung de la Mazière a tremendous salute. 'All present and correct, sir!' he barked. Then he added in a more normal voice: 'You're a sight for sore eyes, sir, you really are! We're glad to have you back — all the noncoms are.'

'Thank you, Papa,' de la Mazière said, forcing a weary grin. 'It's good to be back, I can assure you. How is Hanneman?'

Papa's ancient face lit up. 'Full of piss and vinegar, as usual, sir — if you'll forgive the French, sir. The bone-menders filled him full of pills and we fed him vodka most of the night. This morning at six he was roaring for coffee and his usual dawn rum. Oh yes, he's recovered, sir.'

De la Mazière snorted. 'Sounds like it. God, I wish I had that big rogue's staying power!' Then he dismissed the noncom. 'All right, Papa, let's have a look at the crates.' Briskly the two of them, Diercks with his check-board clutched in one gloved hand, marched across the frozen snow to where the Stukas were lined up, engines already running, as the black-clad mechanics swarmed over the planes carrying out their last checks. In one hour the Wing was scheduled to be airborne. Already, over at the makeshift mess, the Black Knights were drinking their ersatz coffee laced with pervitin and swallowing their dried egg omelettes; it was going to be a long day.

De la Mazière stopped at the first plane and watched keenly as the mechanics fed long belts of gleaming ammunition into the wings, while others wrestled with the 250-pound bombs that would be their load this day. Suddenly he frowned.

'Something wrong, sir?' Papa asked anxiously. He fussed over the planes as if they were his own children. Anything wrong with them was regarded by the chief mechanic as a personal insult.

De la Mazière turned his grey eyes on Papa, his frown deepening. 'Yes,' he said. 'Why the devil are the birds being so heavily fuelled up?' He pointed at the nearest Stuka, its wheels half sunk in the snow. 'The weight of the bombs and the other ammo wouldn't do that, would it, Papa? So it must be the fuel you're pumping into them.'

'That's right, sir,' Papa agreed. 'We've topped them up, right to the limit.'

'But why? Today's flight plan, according to Major Baron Karst, won't entail a round trip of more than — say — one hundred kilometres. Why so much juice?'

Now it was Papa's turn to be puzzled. 'Of course, sir — you're right. That much fuel will slow the plane down even more... But sir,' he looked directly at de la Mazière, standing there straight, lean and severe in his black leather jacket against the background of the wintry field, 'it was a direct order from Major Karst.'

De la Mazière looked thoughtful. Then he snapped, looking at his wristwatch, 'All right, Papa, let's get this thing on the road. Take-off at zero eight hundred — on the nose. See that the fuel tanks are reduced by one third. At the double now!'

'At the double, sir!' Papa Diercks echoed heartily, relieved that he was not going to get a bollocking from the CO this particular morning. He saluted and bustled off, leaving de la Mazière to stare pensively at the horizon, already flickering pink with gunfire. Abruptly he turned and stalked back to the noisy mess. Something fishy was going on and he wanted to know what.

The place was thick with cigar smoke and the heavy scent of fried dried egg. Pilots were jostling each other in the cramped room, eyes already dilated and flashing with the drug pervitin, talking and gesticulating excitedly as they discussed the morning mission, coffee cups in their free hands, flatmen circulating freely. It was a scene that de la Mazière had seen a thousand times before, only in the old days the rotgut had not circulated so openly. But this was 1944 and all their nerves were bad. He pushed through the throng to where Major von Kramm was leaning against the peasant stove, eyes already glittering with drink and drugs, drinking straight from his first flatman of the day.

He caught de la Mazière's look and said heartily: 'Don't worry, sir — just a little of my personal cough mixture. Got a terrible chest.' He coughed dramatically.

De la Mazière grinned. 'You'll probably have a terrible liver, too, Pegleg, if you go on hitting the sauce like that.'

'Don't have livers on the funny farm, sir,' Pegleg answered promptly, but he corked his bottle. 'Just little sieves. Only trouble is that you piss in five directions at the same time!'

'Listen, Pegleg,' de la Mazière said, steering him away from the others, 'what's going on? Why are the crates juiced up like that — right to the top, eh? Come on, spit it out. You know everything that goes on here.'

Pegleg winked solemnly. 'Wooden eye, stay open,' he said, using the old phrase for caution. 'That's the good word.'

'And what's that supposed to mean?'

Pegleg indicated Karst, standing at the far end of the mess by himself. 'For the two days you were missing, Colonel, Karst had the crates juiced up all the time — and his own personal bedroll stowed away in his own plane as well.' His usual grin vanished from his coarse, flushed drinker's face. 'My guess is that if the weather hadn't been so lousy, we would have been long gone.'

'Gone where? To support the Hungarians?'

Pegleg shook his head. 'No — home to Mother.'

De la Mazière gasped. 'Do you mean Karst intended to take the Wing back to the Reich?'

'Something like that,' Pegleg said, avoiding his gaze, fumbling with his flatman.

Face flushed with rage, de la Mazière pushed his way back into the crowd of pilots, automatically noting the loud ones with their horse-laughs and noisy comments, the silent ones huddled in corners, the old ones, the young ones, the ones who were reaching the end of their tether, till he was in the centre of the room. '*Silence in the knocking shop!*' he called, using the traditional cry. 'Let's have some hush, please!'

Gradually the chatter died away and his pilots stared at him, wondering what he might have to say. It was not customary for the Old Man to make a speech at this time of the morning.

De la Mazière let them wait, his grey eyes scanning the soft innocent faces of the greenbeaks; the flushed, drunken, cynical faces of the retreads. 'I have this to say to you,' he commenced, as outside the towing vehicles started to drag the Stukas towards the crude runway cleared in the snow, Papa Diercks fussing over the planes like an old mother hen. 'We are of the SS. You know our motto, comrades. *Loyalty is Our Honour.*' He shot a bitter look at Karst, who was staring over their heads with unfocused eyes. 'And that is not just a smart saying, dreamed up by someone in SS Headquarters in Berlin. It means exactly that. If we abort a mission, break off an attack prematurely, pretend an engine failure, refuse to go in because the flak is too intense —' he shrugged angrily — 'oh, one of a hundred reasons for not pressing home an attack to the limit, we are being disloyal to our comrades on the ground ... and our honour is lost. Do you understand? We of the SS, Germany's élite, are being dishonoured — *by ourselves*!'

One or two of the retreads looked down at their flying boots as if embarrassed. Most of the greenbeaks simply looked bewildered, wondering what this sudden harangue was about. Karst, to whom it was addressed, hardly seemed to be listening. His eyes still remained fixed on that distant horizon known only to himself.

'This morning you've had hot coffeet, eggs and bread — and, by the look of your faces, a good swig of sauce too,' de la Mazière continued bitterly. 'Your stomachs are full and your nerves are being soothed with booze. But what about the poor stubble-hoppers out there in their freezing holes? They'll have been lucky if they got a crust of bread and a drink of snow-water, after being out all night at temperatures which would freeze the eggs off the lot of you. You have special privileges because you are the élite. Now make sure you pay the price for those privileges, even if it costs you your miserable shitting lives!'

He paused for breath, chest heaving angrily, cheeks flushed, while his pilots waited, suddenly deflated and miserable in spite of the drugs and the drink.

'We will continue to support General von Prittwitz's XXX Corps — to the bitter end,' he went on. 'If the stubble-hoppers succeed in breaking through to Slovakia, good, we will have contributed to that success. If they don't...' He shrugged eloquently. 'Too bad for them — *and for us*! But there will be no running away for the 1st SS Stuka Wing. From now on there will be no extra fried sausage for us. Is that absolutely clear, gentlemen?'

There was an awkward shuffling of feet, but some of the greenbeaks muttered, 'Clear, sir.'

'Good,' de la Mazière snapped. 'Right — let's not waste any more time. To the planes! *Los*!'

The men started to leave the room, dragging on their leather flying helmets, tucking away their flatmen, slipping their maps into the big pockets of their overalls. De la Mazière waited by the door as they filed out. Karst came level with him. For an instant their eyes met. Suddenly a cold finger of fear traced its way down the tall Colonel's spine. There was no mistaking that look in Karst's dark fanatical eyes — the look of death. Sooner or later Karst would attempt to kill him; there was absolutely no doubt of it. Then he was gone, after the rest.

Five minutes later, what remained of the 1st SS Stuka Wing was airborne, hurrying westwards towards the pass through the High Tatras, rapidly becoming black dots against the hard blue wash of the winter sky until they disappeared altogether. Down below Papa Diercks crossed himself, said his usual short prayer, not caring that his mechanics were watching him, and allowed himself the first drink of the day from his precious flatman. It would have to last him till they came back. For a few minutes he remained there on the wind-swept field, while the others hurried back to the warmth of the huts, staring at that immense empty sky, wrapped up in his gloomy thoughts, half guessing now what had gone on between Karst and the Old Man.

It had ended like this in the Old War too. After all the glory, the tremendous victories, the fine parties, they had drifted into drugs and drink, with Fat Hermann, their last CO, snorting coke before breakfast. There had been the accusations and counter-accusations, the threats and broken promises, the sudden desire to look after number one. That November so long ago, everything had suddenly fallen apart; they had gone their separate ways without so much as a handshake. That was how the Red Baron's famed Richthofen Squadron had come to a final end.

Papa Diercks frowned. Would the 1st SS Stuka end in the same way? Once, back in the good old days of 1940, the bold young Black Guards had sung a boastful song: *'We shall march on though ruins surround us!'* Now those ruins did surround them at last. Germany was on her knees and the war in the East was virtually lost. Would they still continue to march?

But there was no answer to that overwhelming question. Abruptly overcome by a sense of total depression and gloom, the old white-haired mechanic turned and began to trudge back to the huts, seeing and hearing nothing. On the horizon the sky began to burn.

BOOK 2: *THE BATTLE OF RUZOMBEROK PASS*

CHAPTER 1

The Stuka shuddered violently. In a flash it had been thrown fifty metres upwards, swaying and trembling so that every rivet howled under the strain. The mobile Soviet flak below was firing all out. The planes were hurtling through brown puffballs of exploding smoke, their centres tinged a violent cherry-red.

'Shit on the shingle,' Hannemann growled, vinegar-soaked bandage wrapped around his head under his flying helmet. 'You'd think the Popov bastards would have a bit of sympathy for a bloke with a head like mine... Have I got a beaut of a headache!'

De la Mazière grabbed the stick just in time as another exploding shell blasted the aircraft to port. 'If those Ivan gunners down there get any more accurate,' he cried over the noise, 'you'll have a beaut of an arse-ache too!'

Now the Wing, divided into two groups, were heading down towards the Ruzomberok Pass. Karst's group with the bombs were in the lead. They would scatter the flak guns and their infantry screen. Then de la Mazière's tank-busters would come in to deal with the T-34s that were threatening von Nagy's right flank, as they had been constantly over the last twenty-four hours. Soviet High Command had obviously realised the importance of the Ruzomberok Pass, too. If the Russians could take it before von Nagy got through, they would be able to cut off the rest of XXX Corps in Poland. It would be mass slaughter, with von Prittwitz's infantry trapped with their backs to the High Tatras.

De le Mazière watched as Karst's group went in. Guns were spurting flame the whole length of the approach to the pass. His trained eye told him the mobile gunners were old heads. They weren't using tracer, so the oncoming Stuka pilots would not be able to spot them; there were none of the usual strings of glowing beads to warn the approaching pilots. Karst waggled his wings. Next moment he had flipped over on his back and was falling out of the sky in that terrible death-defying dive. In a tight chain, the rest of his group followed him: nine planes going all out, hurtling downwards at an impossible angle.

The flak was tremendous. Black puffballs and bursts of angry flame everywhere. Time and time again that awesome chute of death was completely obscured by smoke and fire. But Karst's greenbeaks seemed to bear a charmed life. They went racing on and on, the valley floor looming up to meet them at a frightening rate.

De la Mazière swallowed hard, instinctively tightening his grip on the stick, beads of bright sweat gleaming on his forehead. 'It's time to brake, Karst,' an urgent little voice screamed within him. 'Brake, man! *Brake*!'

Karst's plane seemed to stop in mid-air. A myriad black eggs tumbled from its belly and then the Stuka was roaring upwards once more. Plane after plane released its bombs on the flak wagons below, effortlessly tossing the five-ton armoured vehicles into the air as if they were toys.

De la Mazière groaned. The third Stuka was hit. In an instant it was a flaming torch, spewing clouds of oily black smoke. The canopy was thrown back. The gunner tumbled out. A burst of white, and his chute opened. But the pilot was trapped. He couldn't clear the cockpit. Horrified, de la Mazière watched as the scarlet flames rose higher and higher around the pilot.

Suddenly the Stuka went into its death dive, roaring down at 500 kmh. A split second later, it struck the valley floor and disintegrated.

Now it was their turn. As Karst's group flew away, a couple of the Stukas trailing black smoke behind them, limp fingers against the hard blue sky, de la Mazière prepared for his attack. He had that familiar feeling of loneliness, of exposure, as he viewed the burning flak wagons and the line of Ivan tanks beyond. Had Karst knocked out all the flak so that they could concentrate on the tanks? Smoke was drifting everywhere; some of the tanks could still be hidden down there and his Stukas would be easy meat for the enemy gunners when they came in for their low-level strike. He pressed his throat-mike.

'Johann One to all,' he barked, not taking his eyes off the ground for an instant. 'You retreads know what to do if you spot any flak. You greenbeaks, let them have a burst from your cannon. Might get the Popovs rattled and put them off their aim. All right — *Hals und Beinbruck*!... ATTACK! ... ATTACK! ... ATTACK!'

De la Mazière threw his plane into a dive. Weaving violently, he headed for the nearest tank concentration. Scuttling like disturbed beetles from under a log, the T-34s broke out into the open. Tracer started to zip past the canopy like lethal hail. He ignored it. It was only machine-gun fire. The ground loomed ever closer. There were at least a dozen T-34s to his immediate front.

A pulse throbbed in his temple. Suddenly he was breathing in short, sharp gasps. The old exhilaration of the kill overcame him. Adrenaline was speeding through his bloodstream at a tremendous rate. Abruptly his eyes were absolutely, totally keen. He could feel every sense more sharply than ever before. His heart filled with jubilation.

He spotted the command tank. Popov communications were primitive: instead of radios they used flags — and there was the T-34 commander, standing bolt upright in his turret, waving his little flags to scatter his scared crews like some peacetime naval signaller.

'All right, boy-scout,' de la Mazière muttered grimly, 'put this up your shorts!'

Zooming in at ground height, pulling out of that awesome dive at last, he went after the command tank. 'Twist and turn,' he commanded himself. On both sides flak guns opened up at him. Suddenly the Stuka was being buffeted violently, as if punched by gigantic fists. 'Don't worry … keep weaving…' A burst of flame shot up in front of the cockpit. He was blinded momentarily, listening to the shrapnel tap against the armoured glass. He was through an instant later. The command tank was still there. His heart leapt.

'Straighten up,' he ordered himself. 'Forget the flak … *straighten up!*' Now the command tank was directly centred in his sights, the frantic Russian still waving his absurd flags while the other tanks scuttled obediently away. De la Mazière took a huge breath to control his irregular breathing. His nerves were tingling electrically. He'd never felt more alive.

'NOW!'

He throttled back, lowered the flaps and pressed the button almost in the same instant. The Stuka trembled violently. It was as if it had just run into a brick wall. The rivets howled under that terrible pressure. Suddenly the white blur of his armour-piercing shell was hurtling towards the command tank. There was a tremendous searing flash. De la Mazière caught one last glimpse of the T-34 commander in his turret, a blackened shape against the leaping flames. Then he was roaring through a black mushroom of smoke erupting into the sky, steel splinters from below ripping and rapping against his fuselage.

His Stukas were weaving in from all sides to tackle the panicked steel monsters now scattering for cover. Here and there the Russian tank crews kept their heads long enough to fire smoke in a desperate attempt to confuse the Fritzes. But there was no stopping the tank-busters. Retreads and greenbeaks alike, they went howling in, flaps down, throttling back almost to stalling speed, long 37mm cannon pounding sudden death and destruction. They went in from all sides, back, front and rear, looking for the T-34s' weak spots. The Russian tankers tried to offer them their front, the T-34's strongest side. But there was no respite for the hard-pressed Russians. The Black Knights knew exactly what they were looking for: the blue burst of smoke in a white cloud, which indicated an engine running, the T-34's most vulnerable spot.

Engine after engine was hit. With sudden spurts of flame, the AP shells penetrated the thin armour above the engine, igniting tracer ammunition in the crippled tank's locker so that it went zig-zagging in crazy profusion right into the burning sky.

Twice more de la Mazière dived in and both times he was successful. Two more shattered burning T-34s lay behind him, their tracks sprawled out in the charred snow to their rear like severed limbs. But then two red lights started to flicker on his instrument panel, indicating that he had stoppage in both cannon. He cursed and pressed his throat-mike. 'Johann One to Johann Two. Must abort mission. Carry on, Johann Two. Take over, please…'

Johann Two, otherwise known as Pegleg, chuckled sarcastically over the radio. 'And who was talking about never aborting a mission, eh? Taking over now. God in heaven, they send you to the funny farm for doing things like this! Over.'

'Johann Two, I'll get you some more tin for this one. Over.'

'Wouldn't know what to do with it, Johann One. Got a drawerful of the stuff already... *Ende.*'

Even the old cynical retread was feeling the thrill of the chase. He threw his plane out of the sky. Sirens screaming, the engine howling, going full-out, he hurtled down towards the pass already scattered with the crippled hulks of blazing Russian tanks. Beneath him the firs flew past on either side until they became a solid green blur against the white of the snow. Dark running figures appeared to his right. Tiny spurts of scarlet flame. The Popovs had obviously infiltrated infantry onto the heights. The Hungarians would have to be warned later. But first the tanks...

'Come on, you bitch!' he chortled, carried by the heady excitement of that great dive. Lights winked a brazen copper. A flak wagon had scuttled from the rocks at the edge of the battlefield. Abruptly the air in front of him was peppered with whirling angry balls of black smoke. The Stuka rocked violently. Tracer rushed in furious curves towards him, gathering speed by the instant. Dazzling lights blinded him. The whole floor of the pass was aflame.

Pegleg laughed crazily and opened the throttle even wider. It was the Popovs' last desperate attempt to save their tank force. They must not be allowed to escape. It was the funny farm for them this day. 'Here I come, Ivans — the friendly fellow in the white coat driving the rubber van!' He jerked back the stick and levelled out.

He was pressed back hard against his armoured seat by the G-force, his ears popping madly, stars exploding in front of his eyes, face smashed like a pudding against the bones by that terrific pressure. Shells exploded to left and right. The Stuka reeled. Smoke filled his nostrils. Had he been hit? No, the Stuka was answering the controls immediately.

A T-34 loomed up out of the fog of war. He hit the button. The shell streaked in white fury towards the Russian tank. It clanged against the base of the turret. For a moment the metal glowed a frightening dull purple. Inside the crew would be petrified, he knew, as that purple finger traced its way along the outside, trying to find a way in. If it did, they would be torn to bits, flung against the sides in a red dripping gory paste. '*Mincemeat*, Popovs!' Pegleg screamed madly. 'That's what you'll be — *mincemeat*!'

The shell howled away, the turret intact. But it had had its effect. The cover was thrown up. As Pegleg went roaring above the tank, frightened Russians began to emerge, waving white flags. Abruptly the survivors were abandoning their vehicles on all sides, waving anything white, fluttering shirts and vests furiously at the sinister black hawks of death hovering above them.

'They're surrendering, sir,' Slack-Arse gasped over the intercom. 'The whole turd-eating bunch of them are surrendering!'

De la Mazière was circling over the scene, watching the results of his planes' action. A huddle of dark figures stood in the ring of stalled and burning tanks. Slack-Arse was right, he observed; the Popov crews were surrendering. Then he spotted the Hungarians: a long line of cavalry, labouring through the snow in single file. They were standing in their stirrups, fur hats raised as if they were cheering. He waggled his wings in acknowledgement and dragged the black shadow of his Stuka across their white upturned faces as he flew on.

Then he was among his triumphant pilots, the air suddenly full of their excited cries and shouts of triumph as they congratulated each other on their 'kills'. He let them have their moment of victory, as he zoomed over the battlefield with its burning tanks and huge black holes, the bodies of the dead sprawled out in the snow on all sides. There was no doubt about it. The Popovs were either dead or had surrendered. Their attempt to cut off von Prittwitz's XXX Corps had failed. The link between the Corps and the Hungarians had been maintained at the cost of one Stuka downed and two damaged. A small price to pay. Tonight he would write to the dead men's relatives.

Suddenly he felt the excitement drain away. He felt unutterably weary, physically and mentally exhausted. Perhaps it was the thought of the dead men. He didn't know. All he knew was that they had been in actual combat a mere twenty minutes, yet he felt as if it had been twenty hours. It was time to return to base.

He pressed the button of the R/T. 'All right, cut the cackle,' he ordered briskly, trying to hide the weariness in his voice. 'Battle's over — for today at least. Let's go home. Over and out.'

He hauled back the stick and started to rise. Obediently the others followed him, the chatter ceasing at once. At one thousand metres they formed up and turned eastwards.

Within seconds they were just black spots on the horizon. Then they were gone for good, their work of death and destruction completed for the day.

Deep in the Ruzomberok Pass, the Hungarian cavalry ploughed on through the deep snow, twin jets of white smoke ejected at regular intervals from their horses' nostrils. Watching them from the heights, that lone standing figure slapped her monstrous animal knout against her boot in angry, menacing silence…

CHAPTER 2

The door of the hut was flung open unceremoniously and the icy wind, laced with snowflakes, came surging in. Instantly there were angry cries from the men huddled around the tiled stove of 'Shut that shitting door!' and 'Watch the light, willya?'

It was Papa Diercks standing there, his shoulders powdered with snow, a big grin on his wrinkled old face as he kicked the door closed and staggered forward with his case. 'Compliments of General von Prittwitz,' he announced and set the box on the rough wooden table in the centre of the smelly, smoke-filled hut. 'For the NCO corps of the 1st SS Stuka Wing... From his nibs personally.'

Hannemann looked up from his privileged place closest to the merrily crackling stove, feet bare as he attempted to remove the accumulated dirt from beneath his toenails with the point of a captured Russian bayonet. 'What is it?' he grunted. 'The Führer's collected speeches? Or the thoughts of Reichsführer SS Heinrich shitting Himmler?'

Papa's faded old eyes twinkled in the light reflected from the 'Hindenburg candle', their only source of light now. 'What a way to talk to a senior noncom, who could be your very own father.'

'*Father*?' Slack-Arse sneered from where he was running a taper down the side-seams of his shirt, trying to kill the white lice with which it was infested. 'Old fart-guts here didn't have a father — he was created by spontaneous combustion. They just found him one day, fully grown at fourteen, playing chief bull at a home for young whores. Have yer never noticed the length of Hannemann's tongue, Papa?'

There was a rumble of lazy laughter, then someone asked, 'Well, what have you got there, Papa?'

'*This*!' Diercks pulled the first bottle from the straw backing. 'Sauce, comrades — real Polacki vodka, calculated to remove the lining from anybody's tonsils toot-sweet, as the Italians say! *Nastrovya pan*! Up the cups. The night's gonna be —'

The rest of his words were drowned by a delighted yell from Hannemann, followed by hoots and cries from the rest, as Papa started to pull out bottles and toss them into their eager paws.

'Papa is this something!' they cried, biting off the caps in their eagerness. 'After one bottle per man, per week, *per-haps*!'

Solemnly Hannemann bit off the top of his bottle — glass, cap and all — and, after spitting out some glass fragments, took a long and deeply satisfying slug. 'Like mother's milk, Papa,' he announced. 'Goes down like nectar!'

'There's more, Hannemann!' Diercks cried, pulling two cases of cigars from inside his shabby old greatcoat and flinging them around the room. 'And there's a whole case of Old Man canned meat outside for later when you're hungry! Now what d'you say to that, comrades?'

Hannemann grabbed the front of his pants with his free hand, vodka trickling down the stubble of his big chin. 'Can't yer guess? Firewater, cancer-sticks and Old Man! Get me a woman — and Frau Hannemann's handsome son can die happy!'

Papa Diercks grinned. ''Fraid they haven't canned women, yet, Hannemann, but they're working on it.'

A delighted Hannemann didn't seem to hear. Flushed by the drink and the sudden excitement of this unexpected surprise, he said, looking around their faces in the glowing flickering light, 'Did I ever tell you 'bout the pavement pounder I met outside the Lehrter Bahnhof in Berlin — the one with four tits?'

'Yes,' Slack-Arse said mournfully, 'but no doubt you're gonna tell us about it again.'

'That's right. Hey, Papa, toss me one of those lung torpedoes you have and tuck back yer ears. This is something, believe you me. Well…'

Papa Diercks threw Hannemann a cigar and pulled up his greatcoat collar again. They were down to theme number one — sex. This one night, at least, they would be happy. He beamed at them and then slipped out into the night again unnoticed; he had to deliver the other case that von Prittwitz's headquarters had sent up with their meagre rations for the officers.

The 'goodies', he knew, were in part a reward for the successful warding off of the Soviet tank attack the previous day. But that wouldn't be the real reason for the splendid gift. There was something else brewing, he knew it in his old bones.

For a minute, the old man with the heavy crate on his skinny shoulder paused in the gently falling snow for a breather, gaze turned up to the velvet night sky studded with a myriad silver stars. Somewhere there was the soft rumble of artillery, and not far off a Popov machine gun was chattering like an angry woodpecker.

It hardly seemed possible that somewhere or other those same silver stars looked down on a part of the world where all was not snow, savagery and sudden death. He shook his old white-thatched head. At least this one night his boys were happy. He trudged on through the falling snow.

Colonel de la Mazière faced his officers in the tight mess. Once it must have been some hunter's peacetime lodge. There were antlers on the log walls and the mounted head of a moth-eaten black bear, on which, predictably, one of the greenbeaks had placed his cap at a rakishly tilted angle. Presumably there were still bears in the High Tatras; they were high enough and remote enough, too.

'*Meine Herren*,' he began, with unusual formality, so that Pegleg frowned and Karst looked worried, knowing that such formality went only with difficult ops. 'Tomorrow General von Prittwitz of XXX Corps is going to roll his celebrated "goose-egg" into the Ruzomberok Pass.'

Above an excited burst of chatter from the greenbeaks, Pegleg cracked, 'Let's hope the General hard-boiled it!' He guffawed hugely at his own poor attempt at humour.

De la Mazière's tense face cracked into a wintry smile and Pegleg suddenly noticed just how much these last few days had taken out of the Old Man. There were fine wrinkles around his eyes which hadn't been there before and his cheeks seemed even more sunken than ever. A nerve ticked regularly at the side of his face. He looked like a man under severe nervous pressure, who was keeping himself going only by the sheer effort of iron willpower.

'Let us indeed, Pegleg,' de la Mazière agreed. 'It's certainly going to be a tough operation in this winter weather, and hampered as it is by the civvies.' He pushed aside the mugs and glasses set on the dusty table in front of him and drew two straight lines in the dust. 'The pass,' he said, 'with the mountains to both sides. Up here…' he marked an X at the top of the pass, 'are von Nagy's cavalry, already recceing the exit to the pass — so far, fortunately, without meeting any opposition. Here,' another mark, 'the main body of von

Prittwitz's XXX Corps ... with the civilians here. Now this is what the General intends to do tomorrow at first light. He will feed in Gross's 10th Infantry to back up the cavalry. Behind them will come Deutscherl's Bavarians — they're in better shape than the 10th — and the civvies. In the rear will come the rest of von Nagy's cavalry, keeping the Popovs at bay the best they can. Is that clear?' He paused to let his words sink in as the officers stared down at his markings on the dusty table. Then he went on: 'The General's aim is to ensure that he has strong defensive forces at the entrance to the pass, and to some extent at the exit — though of course he is not expecting any trouble in that sector. It is his hope to be able to move the whole force through the pass between dawn and dusk tomorrow. It will be nip-and-tuck, especially with the civilians.'

Again he paused. There was no sound in the room save the heavy breathing of his officers and the gentle hiss of the brass samovar in the far corner, as it boiled purposelessly; for there was no more tea left. Their last drink tonight would be plain hot water.

'Now what is our role in this operation?' De la Mazière answered his own question. 'I shall tell you. We have twenty planes actually fit to fly. That force will be divided between myself and Major Karst.' He nodded in the Baron's direction; but the Baron's face remained as dark and brooding as before, wrapped up as he was in a cocoon of his own sombre thoughts. 'I shall cover the van to act as von Nagy's flying artillery, just in case. Karst, you will take the rearguard. Once the Popovs see us moving into the pass in strength, they will obviously send in their armour. Clear?'

There was a mumble of agreement from the others and Pegleg chortled, 'Well, it'll be a change, won't it? They tell me those Czechs and Slovaks, or whatever they are over there, make a damned good beer — and their womenfolk have tits like melons!' He shook his head in red-faced good humour. 'You can do that between them and you'd think you were smothered in fine silk pillows!'

Nobody laughed at the sally. They were all too preoccupied by what the Old Man had just revealed to them.

De la Mazière looked at Karst. 'What do you think, Major?'

Karst looked at him directly for once, dark eyes glowing with fear and anger. 'It is a perfectly impossible plan, sir,' he rasped. 'Totally out of the question!'

'Why?' de la Mazière asked with deceptive softness.

'Because you are leaving out the fact that not only will the Soviet armour move into the attack, once they spot the Corps is pulling out, but the Red Air Force will move in, too. They'll swamp the pass with those damned Yaks of theirs. It will be an absolute massacre with all those civvies and soldiers packed in down there. Slaughter, mass slaughter, will be the result.' He stopped suddenly, chest heaving with pent-up rage, hands clenched to white-knuckled fists.

De la Mazière took his time, his face impassive though his brain was racing. He knew the terrible effect Karst's words could have on his pilots. Day after day they had been subjected to almost unbearable mental and physical strain. On short rations and in that mind-numbing cold, they had flown mission after mission, constantly fighting off the ever-present fatigue, trying to keep their reactions razor-sharp; for if they let their concentration slip one brief moment, it might well mean the end. Now, publicly, Karst was sapping their will to go on, eroding their ability to continue under these terrible conditions of the Eastern Front. For all of them knew that there was only a one-in-ten chance that they might escape from the Soviet trap.

But could he challenge Karst in the open like this? By now he knew the dark-eyed Major for what he was: a seeker after glory and high office, but with a coward's heart all the same; one eye always on the main chance, so long as there was no risk to himself. A public confrontation, though, would have all the officers taking sides, and that would be fatal. How was he going to do it, without incurring disaster?

For one long moment the two of them faced each other across that dust-covered table, fists clenched, as deadly enemies, as if they were each fighting for a different side, murder in their eyes.

The knock on the door went unnoticed. There was no sound save the hiss of the samovar. The knock came again, louder this time.

Pegleg shook his head as if waking up from a heavy sleep. 'Come!' he bellowed.

Still de la Mazière and Karst and the rest did not move. They remained frozen into position, like bad actors at the end of the third act of some cheap melodrama. Again there was the knock.

'Heaven, arse and cloudburst!' Pegleg cursed, stumping across to the door, his wooden leg squeaking audibly, and flinging it open. 'Holy strawsack!' he cried as he saw Papa Diercks standing there, crate in his arms, bottles sticking out of both pockets and a case of cigars clenched between his chin and chest, his skinny shoulders covered in snow. 'Papa Diercks — Father shitting Christmas himself.' He took the cigars and then as a quick afterthought a bottle from the noncom's pocket. 'Come on in, Papa — you've arrived just in shitting time!'

Papa Diercks stumbled into the tense room, blinking in the sudden light...

Slowly, not seeming to notice the biting cold, de la Mazière walked across the field. Behind him in the hut they were getting noisily drunk, as he had ordered them to do, on von Prittwitz's gift of vodka. 'And the condemned man *drank* a hearty breakfast!' Pegleg had cried loudly, giving him a huge wink. That had started it. Karst's outburst — or was it a challenge? — had been forgotten. Now all of them, retreads as well as greenbeaks, were getting stinking drunk. In the morning they would be lining up outside the oxygen-cylinder shack to have a snort of pure oxygen to clear their befogged brains and rid them of their shocking headaches. Now they would be seeking oblivion.

He frowned. How they had all changed! Once, when they had been young in the good days of 1940, they had been careless, eager, always ready for a scrap in the Holy Cause of a Greater Germany. Even Karst, fanatic that he was, had affected a riding crop, breeches and a monocle, although his vision was perfect. They had all had style and swagger in those days. Now the old eagerness had vanished. They had become reluctant, careful, even cowardly. Greenbeaks and retreads alike, they were primarily concerned with survival.

'*Survival for what?*' asked a little voice at the back of his brain. If Germany lost this war, would life be worth living? They were branded twice over: they were German and they were SS. And de la Mazière, walking there in the sad slow flakes of falling snow, knew what the Popovs would do with any member of the Black Guards who fell into their hands.

He passed the NCOs' hut. They were singing lustily now, voices thick with drink, happy for a few hours before the grey reality of another day at war caught up with them again. '*And the mate at the wheel had a bloody good feel at the girl I left behind me…*' Hannemann bellowed drunkenly, and de la Mazière could just visualise his brick-red face dripping with sweat as he took another mighty swig of rot-gut in between the stanzas of the cynical old ditty. He shook his head and wished he could get joyously drunk like that. But he couldn't.

He walked on.

Before him, outlined a stark black against the silver gloom, he saw his birds. The old Hawks of Death. Once they had been all-powerful, all-conquering, symbols of the might of the New Germany, in the van of that great National Socialist crusade to purge the decadent Old Continent of its vices and its tired, weary old ways. Now they were as old and as tired as Europe.

He stopped beside one of the Hawks and slapped its cold metal side affectionately. 'Hello, you old devil,' he whispered, as the snow drifted down softly and started to settle on his shoulders. 'Don't let me down tomorrow, will you?' There was a note of pleading in his voice.

For several minutes he remained there next to the machine, which was all he had left after five long years of war; then slowly he started to walk back to his quarters, shoulders hunched as if in defeat.

CHAPTER 3

'There goes Major Karst now, sir,' Diercks said, pointing at the blue spurts of the Stuka's exhausts as it raced across the newly cleared path in the snow and hurtled upwards, red identification lights glowing momentarily, before disappearing into the pre-dawn darkness. 'That's the last, sir.'

De la Mazière nodded his thanks. 'Good, Papa, get your people in the trucks. You've got the map reference for the rendezvous in the pass tonight?'

'Scorched earth, sir? Remember the Corps Commander's directive — everything of value to the Popovs has to be destroyed before a unit leaves its current position.'

'I know, I know! Don't fuss so much, Papa. The pilots and air-gunners will take care of it before we set off. Now, off you go before those horrible hairy-arsed Cossacks catch up with you. They have nasty habits with those toothpicks of theirs.'

'That'll be the day when some Ivan in a fur hat puts one over on Old Papa Diercks, sir,' the senior crew chief said boldly, but he saluted quickly enough and hurried off to where the crews were clustering around the trucks which would carry them eastwards with the rest of the moving 'goose-egg'.

De la Mazière smiled and turned to the others, waiting for orders now in the freezing darkness. Just behind him, Hannemann was still holding forth on his favourite subject — sex. '...so her husband said as he burst in, "Hey, what are you doing with yer ugly paws on my wife's tits?" And you know what I said, Slack-Arse? Cool as a cucumber, naturally, I said—'

'Naturally — but get on with it, you lying sod.'

'Well, I said, all sweetness and beauty, "Paws on yer wife's tits, sir? *Never!* Her bosoms just happened to fall out of her dress as she bent down and I was helping her put them back in..." Get it?... Haw, haw, haw!'

'Sergeant Hannemann,' de la Mazière moaned, 'please spare us the lurid details of your sex life — especially at this time of the morning.'

'Just doing as our beloved Führer Adolf Hitler commanded, sir — procreating, furthering the future of the Greater German Folk.'

'You and furthering the future...' de la Mazière began, then changed the subject. 'All right, you pilots and air-gunners back into the hut. I want to speak to you and it's cold enough out here to freeze up even Sergeant Hannemann's notoriously overheated outside plumbing.'

There were a few soft laughs and as the trucks bearing Papa Diercks' ground crews started moving away to join the marching columns of Deutscherl's Bavarians, the men of the 1st SS Stuka walked back into the hut.

De la Mazière waited until Pegleg had closed the door and squatted in the corner with the rest, flatman in hand, before he began. 'All right, comrades, your attention please. Last night, while you were all busy soaking up the suds — and I must say that most of you have faces this morning that only a mother could love — and then only if she needed glasses —'

A few of them laughed and Pegleg told himself the tension of the previous night had been overcome. De la Mazière was his old self. He had made his peace with Karst and the rest who for a while had threatened to split the 1st SS into two enemy camps. He allowed himself a mild drink of the potato schnapps.

'I was puzzling my poor addled brains about today's op. Finally, after a night of turmoil —'

'I know what you mean, sir,' Hannemann interrupted from the rear. 'It was the same with me and the lady whose tits happened to fall out of her dress.'

'*Schnauze*!' half a dozen voices called impatiently. 'Hold yer water, Hannemann!' They were all intrigued by the Old Man's sudden change of heart and the reason he had called them back inside again so unexpectedly.

'I came up with a new plan,' de la Mazière continued doggedly.

'A *new* plan?' they echoed.

'Yes. As Major Karst probably correctly pointed out, once the Ivans know we're all moving into the pass, they'll send up their Yaks. Unfortunately,' de la Mazière gave a little shrug, 'our Stukas are no match for them. So, what can we do about it?'

In the corner Pegleg tensed, flatman untouched in his hand. It was not the answer to de la Mazière's question which interested him, but the fact that de la Mazière was making a conscious effort to hold the Wing together. He sucked his bottom teeth, loose like those of all Stuka pilots, due to the tremendous pressure put on to a pilot's face during their dives. Was the Old Man ripe for the 'friendly fellows', the 'rubber van' and the 'funny farm' now? Didn't he realise that the old loyalties of the SS were long dead, eh?

'So, I thought,' de la Mazière was saying, 'why bring the mountain to Mohammed when Mohammed can go to the mountain? In other words, comrades, *why wait for the Yaks to come to us?*' He stopped and looked around the circles of their faces, most of them appearing frankly bewildered.

Hannemann was the first off the mark. 'You mean ... we should attack them before they attack us?'

'Exactly.'

'But where — and how, sir?'

De la Mazière pushed on eagerly, knowing that he had their undivided attention now. Outside the long column of civilian carts were creaking past the hut, filling the darkness with the crack of bull-whips, the moans and cries of children and the soft shuffle of horses, their hooves wrapped in straw to stop them from slipping on the icy dawn road. 'You know that damned old sewing machine the Popovs send over each dawn to check us out?'

They nodded. They knew he meant the Soviet Rata single-wing reconnaissance plane that had been following the 1st ever since the retreat of the XXX Corps had commenced; it was known as the 'sewing machine' because of the noise of its engine.

'As soon as it's light, it'll be over, knowing that we have nothing in the way of flak to knock it out of the sky, cruising about, looking us over. Now this morning it'll be over, I expect, and it'll see that we've gone. Agreed?'

'Agreed,' they echoed.

'The pilot will radio his base the news and they will immediately assume — correctly — that the 1st has headed for the pass. The burning buildings, in accordance with von Prittwitz's scorched earth order, will tell the Ivan that we've pulled out of here for good. So my guess is that the Popovs will immediately scramble their Yaks and set out to slaughter our people in the pass.'

He looked at his pilots and they stared back at him, obviously puzzled.

'But what if he finds no evidence of our field being abandoned? What if he discovers these miserable huts intact and sees there are still birds on the runway? Then he'll report back that we are still in possession here and those Yaks will remain firmly on the ground, just waiting for us — *to shaft them!*'

'Did you say — shaft them?' Pegleg cried.

'Catch them on the shitting ground!' yelled Graf von Hurwitz, another retread, known as 'Perspex'. 'Great crap on the Christmas tree, it'd be just like the good old days before they put this shitting window in my turnip!' He indicated the glass plate, which gave him his nickname, at the back of his head, the result of a terrible wound in 1941.

'Exactly, Perspex,' de la Mazière responded, eyes sparkling at their sudden enthusiasm. 'We've been running too damned long, *reacting* all the time instead of *acting*. Imagine it, comrades — all those juicy Yaks sitting there at their field at Krakov, just waiting for us to come and make the Ivan bastards eat iron!'

At that moment de la Mazière knew he had them again. They were the same enthusiastic, optimistic Black Knights they had once been in the great days; even the retreads, Pegleg and Perspex, were for it. But what of the 'peasants', the air-gunners, who, as he knew, always viewed their SS officers with suspicion, as men who lived solely for decorations, promotion and glory? But he need not have worried.

Hannemann rose to his feet, lifted one massive haunch and let rip a tremendous burst of fetid wind. 'Gas 'em, bomb 'em, shoot the shit out of 'em, sir!' he roared, his face brick-red with excitement. '*Kill the Popov bastards!*'

'Kill the Popov bastards! Kill the Popovs!' his comrades echoed in hoarse bass unison. '*Kill, kill, kill...*'

'There he is,' de la Mazière hissed over the R/T. 'Complete radio silence now.' He flipped the switch and his radio went dead just as the little Russian plane came swooping in from the red ball of the dawn sun to survey the field below. It began to circle leisurely, just above machine-gun range, knowing that the Fritzes possessed no other anti-aircraft weapons, while high above it in the lightening sky the hawks of death hovered unseen.

On the field below, the damaged Stukas lay in position, as if they were about to take off soon. Smoke trickled a lazy black from the chimneys of the huts, and tiny figures stood around apparently staring upwards, as they always did when the 'sewing machine' made its daily dawn appearance, to watch its performance. The dummies, hastily made of straw from their mattresses and old bits of uniform, looked genuine enough from a height of several hundred feet.

High above, de la Mazière tensed. If the Rata spotted anything wrong, he knew what its reaction would be. It would break off the reconnaissance hastily and head straight back eastwards to Krakov.

The seconds lengthened into minutes. Round and round went the 'sewing machine', circling the field below, outlined a stark black against the ascending sun. Suddenly it made the move that de la Mazière had half-anticipated. It risked going a little lower. Obviously the pilot was not satisfied. Perhaps the absence of movement, the lack of the usual burst of tracer, the unusually still, upturned faces of the Fritzes had unsettled him. But he was definitely diving at a shallow angle to get a better view.

'Keep yer knees crossed, sir, as the Mother Superior said to the nuns,' Hannemann breathed.

'That you can say again, you big rogue,' de la Mazière agreed. 'If those time pencils don't —'

Suddenly from below there was a bright white flash of explosive. In an instant, white and red tracer bullets were zigzagging in crazy disorder towards the Russian plane. The time pencils attached to the pile of ammunition heaped on the centre of the field had worked dead on time. The lethal hail seemed to engulf the little Russian plane and the pilot didn't like it one bit. Frantically he struggled to gain height and escape that furious multi-coloured barrage, weaving from side to side as that lethal morse zipped upwards.

Moments later he was on his way and, listening to the Russian wavelength, de la Mazière could already hear him cursing the '*Fritz artilleria*.' '*Boshe moi — nyet horoscho, nyet horoscho!*...'

'By the Great Whore of Buxtehude, sir, where the dogs shit green peas and the cats piss through their ears, he's bought it! He's bought it!' Hannemann cried excitedly.

De la Mazière nodded, waggling his wings to indicate to the others that they should close up. Obediently they grouped into attack formation, with Perspex on one side of the CO and Pegleg on the other, the two of them grinning like crazy men. De la Mazière waited till they were both watching him; then with his gloved hand he indicated the east and Krakov. Today the Black Hawks would run no more, he reflected, grim-faced and intent. Today it was the turn of the Popovs to do the running...

CHAPTER 4

The sun, blood-red and joyfully warm after the freezing cold night, shone over the white waste below as the Sisters crawled stiffly out of the mountain cave in which they had spent the night and crouched in the rocks above the Ruzomberok Pass.

In silence, Red Rosa surveyed the beautiful sweep of the gleaming peaks of the High Tatras. Behind her the women were preparing the first meal of the day — dried fish, black bread and cold tea, for they dared not light a fire; the Magyars were too close now. She turned her attention to the valley floor. It was filled with tiny black figures, some on horseback, some on foot, with here and there a group of tanks and carts ploughing their way slowly westwards. There was no doubt about it. The Fritzes and their running-dogs the Magyars were in full retreat. She frowned, whacking her bull's pizzle against the side of her boot.

Suddenly Ilona, her current favourite, touched her arm gently and offered her a mug of cold tea, into which she was sprinkling a few precious crystals of hard sugar. 'For you — specially, Comrade Major,' Ilona simpered, rolling her dark eyes meaningfully.

'*Spasiva*,' Red Rosa snapped and dismissed her with a curt jerk of her head. It served no purpose to allow these 'little friends' to get in the way of the serious business of the Great Fatherland's Patriotic War. A few hours of pleasure between the blankets, that's all they were worth; no more and no less.

Moodily she sipped her cold tea, savouring the sweet taste — Ilona had obviously saved the sugar from her own ration — and continued to survey the valley below. The whole Fritz army in Southern Poland was pulling back into Slovakia, and it looked as if the Red Army would be unable to stop them — unless those damned Slovaks could convince the Magyars to defect. In other circumstances Red Rosa would have braved the lion's den herself, boldly shot her way into the Magyar general's HQ and put before him the alternatives — join us or die. But she knew Hungary's situation was too difficult for black-and-white solutions. The Fritzes held Admiral Horthy's son as a hostage in Germany, so no Hungarians would dare deal directly with the Russians. All negotiations with the Magyars would have to be conducted through a third party — in this case, the Slovaks.

Her frown deepened at the thought, and she drained the rest of her tea almost angrily. The 'little friend' was at her side immediately, offering her some dried fish and a hunk of bread.

Red Rosa thrust her aside impatiently. 'I have no time for food now,' she snapped, tossing the mug to the dark-eyed woman who had been her lover for the last three months. 'There are more important things to be done than stuff one's guts with food.'

Ilona caught the mug, her bottom lip trembling as if she might break into tears at any moment.

Red Rosa ignored her. What fools most women were, she told herself, turning away and clambering up the mountainside towards the look-out post. As she climbed she found herself panting a little in the thin air of the High Tatras, and a bitter wind whipped particles of ice against her face in a myriad tiny pinpricks.

'Well?' she demanded of the big burly Sister who was on sentry duty. 'Any sign of them?'

'They must be down there somewhere, Comrade Major,' the look-out reported, after snapping to attention, rifle clutched to her side like a soldier on parade in some peacetime garrison. 'They've been firing signal flares for the last half hour or so. And they've got a patrol out. Look, Comrade Major...' she raised one stiff arm and pointed.

'Stop playing the toy soldier,' Red Rosa commanded. 'Where?'

'There — to the right of those firs.'

Red Rosa sighed. Was there no end to the foolishness of women? Here was Vera, who had personally sliced the genitals off six Fritzes with her cut-throat razor, pouting sulkily now like Ilona just because she had been reprimanded. She slapped her bull's pizzle against her boot. *Boshe moi*, why hadn't she been born a man!

Down to their right, perhaps five hundred metres away, a small patrol of Hungarian cavalry was ploughing heavily through the thick snow, strung out in a long line, the sun glinting on their drawn sabres. Their sweating, gleaming horses bobbed up and down, belly-deep in snow, twin rods of grey spurting from distended nostrils as their riders urged them forward, digging in their spurs.

Hastily Red Rosa flung up her glasses, shielding the lenses with her free hand so that any reflection would not reveal her position. A face slid into the circle of calibrated glass. She adjusted the focus quickly. It became clearer, the soft weakly handsome face of the kind of aristocratic cavalry officer she remembered from old pictures of the days of the Czar. Her lip curled in disgust. But she knew she had no time for such self-indulgence. The Hungarian was definitely after something. Why else would he venture so far from the main body of the Fritz army? She swung the binoculars round, covering the ground to the immediate front of the patrol.

A dark shape was moving through the snow-heavy firs at three o'clock. She could follow his progress easily as the fugitive blundered in panic through the stunted trees, showering down fresh snow in gleaming cascades every time he moved. They were after him; he was their quarry!

She tensed. Could it be their man? But there were supposed to be two of the Slovaks … she watched and waited. If he were wearing a uniform, she would soon know. The fugitive stumbled across an open fire-break. She caught a glimpse of a fat, terrified Slavic face and a soaked khaki greatcoat, completely different in hue from anything the Fritzes or Magyars wore. It was him; it had to be. The messenger from the two Slovak divisions. Hurriedly she swung her glasses back to the Hungarians. They were about two hundred metres behind the Slovak, splitting up into two groups, floundering their way through the snow on both sides of the wood. Obviously they were attempting to encircle the running man. She let the glasses drop to her heavy bosom that shivered beneath her padded jacket like a fat jelly every time she moved.

'Keep an eye on that patrol,' she commanded, mind made up. 'Fire immediately there is any sign of movement from the main body. One shot will do it. *Horoscho?*'

'*Horoscho,*' Vera replied dutifully, broad, homely face beaming now that she was in her beloved commander's good graces once more.

Red Rosa wasted no more time. For such a big, awkward-looking woman, she moved swiftly down the mountainside, sliding and slipping, her face flushed with the exertion, but with breath enough to cry to the women crouched eating at the entrance of the cave like off-shift miners in her native Donetz-Basin, '*Davai, davai*! The enemy are on us! Quick, take up your defensive positions!…'

The Slovak burst out of the trees.

Some fifty metres behind him, the handsome young Hungarian officer rose in his stirrups and waved his sabre above his fur-capped head, the blade gleaming a bright silver in the sun. He yelled something, breath fogging the air. Digging in his stirrups cruelly and jerking at the bit, he urged his panting, sweat-lathered mount after the fugitive.

The Slovak flung a terrified glance over his shoulder. The Hungarian was lying flat over the mane of his mount, sabre thrust out, coming in for the kill. He floundered on, chest heaving as if it were going to burst at any moment, eyes wild with unreasoning panic. Now the only sound was the jingle of harness and the gasping, rasping noises of the exhausted horses.

Behind the rocks, Red Rosa glanced to left and right. Her Sisters were perfectly calm, even that pretty little fool Ilona, each woman with her weapon at the ready, gaze fixed intently on the unsuspecting enemy. Not one of them showed even a trace of fear. She nodded her satisfaction and threw a quick look at the observation post above her. All was quiet up there. The Fritzes and their running-dogs were obviously too intent on making their escape through the pass to worry about what was going on in the heights. She raised her bull's pizzle.

Now the young officer was only metres behind the running man. He raised his sabre. In a moment he would bring it down and cleave the Slovak's head in two. Even at that distance Red Rosa could see the look of triumph on his weakly handsome face.

The Slovak stumbled. Desperately he tried to keep his footing. To no avail. He sprawled full length in the snow, all breath knocked from him, and lay there supinely to await his end. The Hungarian officer tugged fiercely at the reins. His black stallion whinnied with pain. It reared upwards, forelegs flailing the air. The officer raised his sabre over his head, flashing in the blood-red light of the sun. He opened his mouth to reveal bright white teeth and cried something.

Red Rosa slapped the pizzle down against her boot. It was the signal. Fire erupted from along the whole length of the rocks. For one long moment the Hungarian still pranced there on his mount, sabre upraised, other hand clutching the rein tightly, the scarlet stains spreading like a blossoming flower on the breast of his tunic. Next instant he was sliding from his saddle, sabre tumbling from suddenly nerveless fingers, an incredulous look on his stupid face as he pitched head-down into the snow.

What happened next was a massacre. At that range even the worst shot among the Sisters could not miss. That sudden deluge of fire from behind the rocks hosed the cavalry from their horses. They went down on all sides, a confused mass of men and mounts, the horses fighting valiantly to climb back on their feet, their flanks lathered with sweat and blood, while beneath them the dying riders howled in their final agony, crushed by their hooves, while the slugs continued to thud mercilessly into the slaughtered patrol.

It was all over in a matter of minutes. One instant all was confusion, with men and horses falling everywhere and riderless animals plunging away into the distance, manes streaming behind them, eyes wild with terror. Next instant all was brooding silence, broken only by the moans of the dying Hungarian soldiers, peasant boys to a man, snatched from their remote farms to die in this nameless place for a cause they hardly understood.

Red Rosa raised her bull's pizzle. The women stopped firing immediately. As always their fire discipline was perfect.

Anxiously she peered down at the valley floor far below. If the Fritzes had noticed the firing, they showed no sign of it. They continued their progress westwards, toiling through the pass like tiny black insects on some annual migration, gaze fixed on the ground. She nodded her approval. They had got away with it.

'Ilona,' she commanded, 'you and Marika bring in the Slovak — quick now.'

A minute later the two women were back, weapons slung, half-carrying the Slovak, a fat-faced, undersized officer, babbling wildly in a mixture of his own tongue and Russian, his baggy breeches soaked black — but not only with snow. Red Rosa wrinkled her nose in disgust. In his fear the man had soiled himself. Typical South Slav, she told herself contemptuously: all brass bands, beer and pork, and the soft life at any price. Now they would have to learn that one had to pay — and pay dearly — for the privilege of living.

She cut his babbled thanks short. 'You — go behind those rocks and clean yourself up. You are in a disgusting state.'

One of the Sisters giggled, a strange unreal sound in that place of death. Red Rosa swung round on her immediately, bull's pizzle raised, while the Slovak slunk behind the rocks miserably, still babbling to himself. The woman cowered.

Red Rosa ruled with an iron hand. It wouldn't be the first time that she had stripped one of the Sisters naked at twenty degrees below zero and beaten her back to a bloody pulp with that terrible knout for some minor infringement of discipline.

'Funny, eh, comrade? Then I shall give you something to really laugh about. Go and search the bodies of those Magyar pigs. Bring back anything you think we can use. *Davai!*'

The woman bent her head and went reluctantly. Most of the Sisters had been recruited from the *kulak* class and the peasants of that type were still as superstitious as they had been back in the Dark Ages; they hated touching dead bodies without the presence of a priest to ward off the devils.

Red Rosa forgot the reluctant body-searcher and walked over to the cave. 'Bring me the Slovak pig,' she ordered, 'as soon as he is clean.'

Five minutes later he was brought into the cave, recovered from his ordeal a little, but his eyes wide with wonder at this strange company in which he now found himself in the remote mountains. 'Frantek, Major,' he introduced himself with a stiff little bow — as if he were some damned Imperialist officer, Rosa told herself, her disgust mounting once more.

She jerked her thumb. 'Sit,' she commanded.

He sat, the rest of his introduction suddenly halted.

'*Horoscho*, Frantek, Major,' she commenced, her contempt unconcealed. 'What have you to tell me?'

'The two divisions of the Slovak Army in Eastern Slovakia are prepared to rise against the fascists and —'

She held up her big hand for silence and, staring hard at his fat soft face, snapped: 'Don't tell me, Frantek, Major. Once the Red Army has done the dirty work of destroying the Fritz XXX Corps. First things first, *Comrade* Major,' she emphasised the word with a sneer. Once the Red Army took over, all these Balkan Slavs, or whatever they were, suddenly became communists. They knew which side their bread was buttered on. Before her she had an instant communist, she knew it. But he wasn't going to get off that easily. 'Now what does this damned Magyar von Nagy say?' she demanded.

'At first we thought that he was going to come over to us without any trouble,' the Slovak answered. 'We told him that he was not fighting for Russia, but for the independence of his homeland against both German and Russian.'

Red Rosa nodded her approval. That was standard operating procedure with these minorities at first. Then their own people who were loyal communists would be flown in from Moscow, a 'popular national' government would be formed, and before they knew what had happened to them they were being ruled from Moscow. 'Go on. What happened?'

'At the second meeting yesterday he changed his mind. He said he could not betray the Germans. His honour was at stake.' Frantek frowned thoughtfully. 'I think the Germans must have given some assurances that he would have their full support, perhaps planes or something. After I left him, I talked with some of his senior officers. They were still prepared to go along with us, but von Nagy was the stumbling block. They were not prepared to raise their hand against their commander. You must understand, Comrade Major...' He paused, staring at the huge woman with a suspicion of a moustache under her bulbous drinker's nose, then gave her a small smile. 'We who once belonged to the Austro-Hungarian empire have rather antiquated ideas of honour and loyalty.'

Rosa slapped her boot with the bull's pizzle. 'We Soviets have only one loyalty — to the working class of the world!' She glared at him fiercely.

'Yes, yes,' Frantek said hastily. 'Of course. So I left it at that. Unfortunately, on my way to report to you with my assistant Lieutenant Frolik I ran into that Hungarian patrol. They knew nothing of the safe conduct that von Nagy had granted me — and poor Frolik, a cousin of mine by the way, Major, on my mother's side...' The Slovak's words trailed away to nothing. Red Rosa was not listening. He bit his bottom lip and waited, telling himself that it was impossible, even criminal, to be a national of a small power. Always one had to be on one's guard against these rapacious beasts of the great nations.

Red Rosa made her decision. 'So the Hungarians would go over to you if General — er — von Nagy was not in command.'

'Yes, Comrade Major,' Frantek answered dutifully, wondering if he would ever get used to this strange way of addressing everyone as 'comrade'. 'That is my impression from talking to the other Hungarian officers.'

'*Horoscho.*' Red Rosa whacked her bull's pizzle down and made Frantek jump. 'Then we must eliminate General von Nagy forthwith.'

'Eliminate?' Frantek echoed.

Red Rosa looked at him, a smile on her face, but there was no answering light in her dark bold eyes. Slowly she drew one finger across her neck, as if she were slitting it with a knife. 'Like that,' she said.

Frantek shuddered.

CHAPTER 5

It was an old trick, but it worked. Packed tightly together, de la Mazière's group had flown with the clouds scudding in from the west, using them cunningly so that they reached the Krakov base without being seen. Now, with Krakov's great cathedral dominating the sky to their rear, spires pointing upwards like dark accusing fingers, they circled the base carefully.

The stubby little Yaks were lined up side by side on the ground, as if this were peacetime and they were in position ready to be inspected by some high-ranking officer. Mechanics were going about their ordinary business, tinkering with engines, rolling out drums of gasoline, dragging long belts of gleaming yellow ammunition, manhandling stepladders around the craft. All was casual, carefree industry, as if the war were a thousand kilometres away.

'Wow,' Hannemann breathed over the intercom, 'what a bunch o' fat cats! Great crap on the Christmas tree, are we really catching them with their skivvies around their ankles like this?'

De la Mazière took his gaze off the flak gunners lounging around their twin cannon behind the sand-bagged pits. 'It looks very like it,' he said carefully. 'It certainly looks like it.'

'Then what are we waiting for, sir?' Hannemann cried eagerly. 'Let's give 'em the purple shaft while they're still squatting there, arses in the air!'

Hannemann's excited outburst broke the strange spell. De la Mazière reacted at once. He waggled his wings. To left and right, Pegleg and Perspex flashed him an expectant look. He pressed the button on his R/T. 'Gentlemen,' he announced with formal gravity, though his heart was thumping excitedly as of old, 'shall we begin the dance?'

'Bags me the first waltz, sir!' Pegleg chortled.

De la Mazière's tension vanished. He felt icy-cold. '*Attack*! ... *Attack*! ... *Attack*!...' he bellowed and thrust his stick down. The battle had commenced.

The Stukas hurtled down towards the field. Immediately the shocked gunners took up the challenge. Madly fumbling with their dials and gauges, they opened up with light flak. The air filled with long incandescent trails. Red and green tracer shells criss-crossed. Surging through the flak, de la Mazière felt it was just about to hit him between the eyes — but at the very last moment it curved off to one side.

Abruptly guns were firing at the Stukas from all sides. Venomous black puffs. Clusters of hurrying luminous balls of flame. Exploding shells, like flowers unfolding at top speed to reveal that deadly, scarlet-glowing centre. Time and time again that chute of hurtling death vanished into the smoke, and it seemed impossible that they could escape. But they did. Over and over again.

At five hundred metres de la Mazière hauled back on the stick, his shoulder muscles bulging and threatening to burst out of the thin material of his shirt. The Stuka staggered. The G-Force pressed him hard against the seat. His stomach was slammed against his spine. He was pinned there helplessly, gasping for breath like a stranded fish. He blacked out momentarily. Then he had the machine again.

'Line abreast!' he gasped over the R/T.

To left and right his pilots took up their formation. Still the flak pounded them relentlessly, but the Stuka crews seemed not to notice.

'*Hals und Beinbruck!*' de la Mazière yelled and raced in at ground-level, finger hovering over the firing button.

A haystack, covered in snow. Men in earth-coloured blouses running frantically towards it. Two long-barrelled cannon thrusting through the hay and snow. De la Mazière hit the button. His port cannon belched fire. Behind him Hannemann swung his single machine gun round and hosed the haystack with a merciless burst of tracer. The running men whirled round and round in their dying agony like mad ballet-dancers. The haystack went up in a whoosh of flame. De la Mazière caught a glimpse of a headless body still on its feet, then he was hurtling on towards the parked Yaks.

As one the Black Knights pressed their firing buttons. It was like an old-fashioned broadside from a man-o'-war. The prodigious thunderclap of that tremendous barrage rolled back and forth across the valley. A sudden gust like the wind from a gigantic fan swept across the field, whipping up the snow in crazy fury, howling relentlessly down the cleared runway.

Yaks disappeared, were flung into the air like children's toys, slapped down to the ground, burst into flames, disintegrated, slammed against the hangar doors and crumpled as if they were made of tin, exploded, sending a shower of gleaming metal into the burning sky.

Abruptly the Stukas were flying through the rain of silver metal, fragments rapping against their fuselages with a deafening tattoo. An instant later they were climbing in a stiff tight turn, the flak hammering away hopelessly behind them as the field burned.

But the Hawks of Death were not finished yet. De la Mazière reasoned that the Reds would think that was that. They had made enough kills and would fly away, especially as the flak was now alerted. But there were still intact Yaks down there among the blazing wreckage, perhaps twenty or thirty of them. Today, however, the 1st SS Stuka Wing would wreck the whole of the Red Air Force in Southern Poland; they owed it to their comrades in the Army, those poor miserable stubble-hoppers of von Prittwitz's XXX Corps.

He pressed the R/T button. 'We're going in again,' he rasped.

'Holy strawsack, Detlev!' Pegleg gasped, so shocked that he addressed the Old Man by his first name, as he had once done in the good days when they had been carefree young lieutenants together. 'Ain't you had a noseful yet?'

'Hell, no!' de la Mazière answered, carried away by the heady excitement of aerial combat. 'What's up, Pegleg — pants full?'

'Totally! Right down to my frigging ankles, Detlev!'

De la Mazière flung a glance out of the canopy as the planes levelled out. Pegleg was grinning at him. He waved. Pegleg waved back. De la Mazière was overcome by a warm feeling of comradeship. At that moment he could have broken down and wept. What good fellows they were! He hit the R/T button. '*Kameraden der Waffen SS*,' he shrieked with all his strength, carried away by a crazed elation, '*Our honour is loyalty... Angreifen, angreifen!...*' He slammed home his stick and fell out of the sky once again.

At 400kmh he raced downwards, engine howling, sirens going full out. The burning field hurtled up to meet him. The tremendous G-force hammered at him. His Stuka shuddered and vibrated under the tremendous pressure. He thrust the stick forward even more, coaxing every last bit of speed out of the plane. His ears pounded. For an instant control was snatched from him and he blacked out. It was as if the whole world had collapsed. Helplessly he was pressed back against his seat, his mind shrouded in black whirling fog. In a haze he had the feeling that the Stuka had come to life, had an existence of its own, was dragging itself from the control of his sweaty hands on the stick and his feet on the rudder bar. '*Stop it!*' he heard himself screaming hysterically. '*Stop it!... I'm in control!... Stop it!*'

Suddenly he had full possession of his senses once more. Over the intercom, Hannemann was bellowing in naked panic. 'Level out, man! For shit's sake, LEVEL OUT!'

De la Mazière eased back the stick. The plane did not respond. They were hurtling towards death, the ground was only a matter of a couple of hundred metres away. He screamed obscenely and half stood up in the cockpit, feet braced against the floor, heaving with all his strength, shoulder muscles aflame with agony, face purple, eyes bulging from their sockets with that impossible strain.

The Stuka gradually responded. It was coming out of the dive. He heaved again, yelping with pain as red-hot pincers of agony nipped at his shoulder muscles. Ten metres above the snow-covered ground, the Stuka finally levelled out.

'Oh my aching arse, sir!' gasped Hannemann. 'I thought we were for the chop then, sir!'

'Not just yet,' de la Mazière answered through gritted teeth. Then, hitting the R/T button, he bellowed, 'Line abreast — go! *Attack!*'

It was like an old-fashioned cavalry charge. Skimming across the snowfield at ten metres, their props churning the air, trees rushing by in a green blur, they headed straight for the blazing air base once more. The flak-gunners recovered from their surprise quickly. Tracer streamed towards them like glowing golf balls, thickening by the second so it seemed that they were flying straight into a solid wall of burning steel.

De la Mazière's heart leapt. Directly ahead of him was a line of trees. He banked instinctively, hitting full left rudder. Too late. The Stuka's starboard wing clipped the top of a tree with a terrifying bang. But the Stuka kept on going, thrust forward by the momentum of five tons of aircraft racing at 400 kmh.

De la Mazière shook his head. Fear had twisted his guts so that it was only at the very last moment that he prevented himself from evacuating his bowels. Dazed with shock he flashed under a line of high-tension cables. Shells were exploding all around him. The plane was flung from side to side. Oil streamed out from a ruptured line, blinding him as it splashed the canopy. He jettisoned it automatically. The icy cold air slapped him across the face like the punch from a heavyweight. He gasped with shock. But that blast of freezing air woke him from his unreasoning panic.

Now before him the cratered field with shattered aircraft lying everywhere was set out in absolute clarity. To the left he could see a line of Yaks they had not damaged in the first run.

To the right, on the runway itself, two Yaks were hurtling forward, propellers whirling furiously as they tried to take off.

'Hard luck, friends!' de la Mazière yelled and hit the firing button of his 37mm cannon.

The tracer shells spurted from his guns in white fury. They hissed towards the Yaks, trailing smoke behind them. The first shell hit the tarmac and whined off harmlessly. The second struck its target. The second Yak came to a sudden stop, as if it had just run into an invisible wall. Next moment its undercarriage gave way beneath it and it was slithering helplessly on its belly along the tarmac, a furious wake of snow thrown up behind it.

The first Yak took off. It went straight into a vertical climb, directly in front of de la Mazière, shooting up like a rocket. For one long moment its whole underbelly was exposed. The target was perfect. De la Mazière hit the button. The Stuka shuddered with the recoil. Acrid smoke filled the open cockpit. With a slight motion of the stick, wolfish face set in a merciless grin, de la Mazière ran the luminous spot of his gunsight the length of the Yak's guts, knocking great lumps of metal from them.

The Yak appeared to hang there, prop churning the air like an antiquated windmill. Still it did not go into its final dive. *Would the bastard never drop out of the sky?* A flicker of crimson. Smoke was pouring out of the shattered fuselage. Shells were still dancing towards its engine. God in heaven, how tough the brute was!

'Die, damn you! Die!' de la Mazière screamed as he hurtled towards the seemingly stationary Yak on a collision course.

Abruptly the Yak flipped over on its back. Then it was gone, streaming towards the ground like a comet, trailing bits of metal behind it. It hit the tarmac with a tremendous explosion, and was engulfed in a ball of fire.

A hiss of pressurised air told de la Mazière that his shells had given out. His cannon were empty. 'Hannemann,' he yelled above the racket, hoping fervently that his goggles would not fog up in the icy air streaming into the open cockpit, 'I'm out of ammo — it's up to you now!'

'Bandits at three o'clock high!' Hannemann roared back.

'Oh my Christ,' de la Mazière moaned as they sailed across the burning field, leaving the other Stukas behind to complete their deadly work on the surviving Russian planes.

Racing towards them were three Yaks. There was no mistaking that untidy Russian formation as the enemy pilots raced in to help their stricken comrades on the ground. Perhaps they had been on patrol; perhaps they were new aircraft coming to join the frontline squadrons. It didn't matter.

All that de la Mazière was concerned with was that they would soon be attacking him and the unsuspecting Stukas, easy targets for those fast, nimble fighters. And he was virtually defenceless...

Hastily he huddled down deeper in his seat and stiffened his feet on the rudder bar. All his initial fear had vanished. Excitement and determination had taken over, keying up his muscles to their highest pitch of efficiency. He zoomed towards the Yaks.

The Russian leader spotted him. He waggled his wings to signal to the others. They responded immediately. Breaking off their attack on the Stukas dive-bombing the field, they changed direction and raced forward, set on destroying this lone Stuka.

De la Mazière laughed harshly and flung the Stuka into a sudden spiral. The long glittering stream of tracer missed him by metres. Abruptly the world became a mad whirling kaleidoscope. The three Yaks hurtled harmlessly overhead. Next moment they were opening out like a fan, climbing at an enormous rate, intent on falling onto de la Mazière straight out of the sun. He pulled the Stuka out of its dive in the same moment that they flipped over onto their backs and zoomed down. Now he was racing along at tree-top height, surging eastwards and away from the burning field, praying the damaged wing-tip wouldn't let him down. And the Yaks were following. They had seized the bait.

'Hey — you're going in the wrong shitting direction, sir!' Hannemann bellowed in alarm.

'I know ... I know...'

'But what are we gonna do?'

'Pray, Hannemann, pray!'

The first of the Yaks was catching up. In his rear-view mirror, de la Mazière could see the long trails of brown smoke erupting from the plane's wings and the glittering yellow rain of the empties. He stood on the starboard rudder bar, and the Stuka went into a tight right-hand turn. The stream of white-glowing steel from the Yak went hissing past, just missing him.

The Russian hurtled on, so intent on the kill that he overlooked Hannemann manning the Stuka's rear machine gun. But the big red-faced gunner was there all right, drawing the unsuspecting Yak pilot right into his field of fire, the little stubby plane growing ever bigger and easier in the circle of his ring sight.

He waited no longer. 'Now!' he commanded himself and pressed his trigger. At that range he couldn't miss. He fired a full burst right into the Yak's engine, running his slugs up towards the gleaming canopy.

The result was dramatic. The Yak skidded violently to the right, its wing crumpling as if made of paper, then shearing off. It ran the length of the fuselage sending up a shower of violet sparks, slammed into the tailplane and knocked it off. The Yak swept down into an immediate dive, totally out of control, the pilot fighting desperately, face contorted with fear, to open his canopy. Too late! The Yak slapped into a line of thatch-roofed peasant cottages below. Both plane and cottages disintegrated in a burst of flames.

De la Mazière throttled back. The Stuka shook alarmingly. The two remaining Yaks shot over his head. For an instant they filled the sky; he could see every rivet of their oil-stained bellies. Then they were gone, howling straight into the sky, trailing smoke behind them.

He did not wait to see what they would do next. He knew already. They would make a tight turn and come zooming down at him again. He had to get out of here while there was still time. He banked steeply, feeling the Stuka shiver and judder under the strain. The engine howled in protest. For one awful moment he thought the whole plane was going to fall apart...

Now he was round, hedge-hopping, going flat out, keeping as low as he dared, trees zipping past on either side as he attempted desperately to put space between him and the climbing Yaks. In a minute they'd turn. By then he wanted to be almost up to the clouds scudding across his front.

'Here they come, sir!' Hannemann sang out.

He threw a glance in his rear-view mirror. The two remaining Yaks were surging towards him from left and right, machine guns already chattering frenetically, tracer zipping in bright lethal streams towards his tail. Weaving violently, using all his skill, he raced for the cover of the clouds, which suddenly seemed a million kilometres away.

The Yaks were gaining on him. Slugs were hammering against the fuselage. He could feel the cold air rushing in through the holes they had torn in the fabric. He swung to the left. They kept on his tail.

Behind him Hannemann let his paws fall from the machine gun. 'No more ammo, sir!... We've had it!' he yelled.

They were completely defenceless now, de la Mazière reflected grimly.

He pulled back the stick. The Stuka responded at once, climbing in a near vertical dive. Seconds later the plane was being pummelled by a tremendous blast of infuriated disturbed air. He flashed a glance in the rear-view mirror, as a booming noise like the crack of doom battered his ears.

The two Yaks had been over-eager. They had smashed into one another. Now, momentarily, they were locked together. Suddenly they began to fall. Welded together by the force of the impact, they fell in a confused mess, showering sparks behind them. One chute billowed open, then another. Abruptly the two planes tore apart in a fiery burst of angry scarlet flame. Then the air was empty again, save for the two parachutes gently floating down to earth. The Russian pilots had escaped.

'I ... I can't believe it, sir,' Hannemann stuttered in a tiny voice, staring into the empty sky. 'That we got away with it... Thought we were for the chop today.'

De la Mazière swallowed hard, suddenly realising just how weary and drained of energy he was. 'A shitting miracle, Hannemann, that's what it is... Come on, let's go home — wherever home might be tonight.'

The battered old Stuka turned westwards again. The Russian field came into view, tall black mushrooms of smoke everywhere, flecked with cherry-red bursts of flame. But no one was firing at them now. Below there was nothing but burning, shattered wreckage. De la Mazière stared down at the field without interest as they limped on. They had done what they had intended to do, but the knowledge gave him no pleasure. He was too drained.

The first unmistakable shape of a Stuka came into sight; a long way behind it was another, trailing smoke. De la Mazière's R/T set crackled into sudden life. It was Pegleg's voice.

'Hello, Johann One! Hello, Johann One!' he called, jubilation clear even over the air. 'Did we shaft 'em, eh! I counted 'em — sixty Yaks at least destroyed. That's the equivalent of two wings of the Red bastards!'

'Anyone bought it?' de la Mazière forced himself to ask.

'Yes, that poor young shit von Marmagen went hop. Ran right into flying shit. Disintegrated... And behind me old Perspex took a bad burst, wounded in the arm. Complaining as usual, of course. Think he's about ripe for the old funny farm—'

'I heard that, you moth-eaten old cripple,' Perspex burst into the R/T conversation in mock anger. 'I know who wears rubber pants beneath his slacks in case his old fart-cannon lets him down and he shits himself with fear —'

'All right, all right!' de la Mazière cut in with a weary smile. 'Hold your water, the two of you. Let's cut the cackle and see if we can find somewhere to land.'

Gradually the other planes formed up to left and right of the badly battered Stuka. All of them had been hit — lacerated tailplanes, gaping holes in the fuselage, wings and bellies charred with fire or glistening with black oil seeping from punctured engines — but they were still flying. The scars of victory, de la Mazière told himself as they flew steadily westwards. Once again the 1st SS Stuka Squadron had surprised the enemy and snatched victory out of what might have been defeat. Suddenly, in spite of his almost overwhelming weariness, he felt a warm sense of pride in his men. They had beaten the Ivans.

But it would be their last victory.

BOOK 3: *THE DESTRUCTION OF THE 1ST SS*

CHAPTER 1

They shot General von Nagy at eight o'clock precisely that same night.

As was his custom, the Hungarian General ate a frugal supper of Czech *spaetzli* without sauce, drank a single glass of his beloved Tokay (now carefully hoarded), took one last look at the maps in the mobile ops room, bade goodnight to his Chief-of-Staff Colonel Poldi, and then went over to the peasant hut, his billet for the night, where his servant awaited him.

Settling into his warm bunk near the glowing stove, he commenced his habitual nightly read, glasses on the end of his long nose, enjoying this time out of war. By nine o'clock he would be fast asleep. He had always campaigned thus; it was the only way he knew of maintaining one's sanity in a world gone absolutely, completely crazy.

Now he snuggled there happily, old-fashioned stocking nightcap pulled down over his ears to keep the cold out, half-listening to the snowstorm raging outside, following the well-known adventures of Karl May's fictional cowboys and 'Old Shatterhand', his celebrated hero. He still had a whole hour to go before he turned in.

Soft footsteps padded through the thick white curtain of falling snow. A faint yellow light marked the hut. The Hungarian sentries shuffled their feet to keep warm, upturned collars around their ears, rifles slung carelessly over their bent shoulders, hands dug deep in pockets. The tethered horses whinnied softly over to the right in the horse-lines.

Red Rosa parted the snow-heavy bushes behind the hut. 'Ilona ... Vera...' She didn't need to say any more.

Half-crouched, their shoulders sprinkled with snow, the two Sisters advanced towards the door of the hut, tommy-guns at the ready.

Red Rosa waited until they were in position, then made an encircling movement with the bull's pizzle, whispering a curt command.

The two women nodded, crouching one on either side of the door, tense and alert, fingers curling round their triggers. Now the little hut containing the unsuspecting General was sealed off from the rest of the camp. Not that Red Rosa expected any trouble. Poldi had told the Slovak Frantek that there would be no interference from him or his men. But some fool might just blunder into the women and cause trouble among those who did not know that their commanding general was scheduled to be murdered this snowy night.

Red Rosa took one final look at her situation. Then she hesitated no longer. She nodded to the two sisters crouching next to the door. For such a frail-looking woman, Ilona showed surprising strength. One swift kick and the door flew open. Yellow light knifed the white-glowing darkness. Next moment Red Rosa had burst through the open door, followed by her two companions, and was staring down at the old man lying on his bunk. Beneath the woolly nightcap his face looked shrunken without the false teeth that lay in the glass next to the bunk, but he seemed unafraid at the sight of these brutal-looking women in their heavy padded jackets, tommy-guns aimed straight at him.

'Russians?' he asked in their own language. He shook his head sadly. 'So they have betrayed me, eh?' Slowly he lowered his Karl May. 'Who was it? Colonel Poldi or perhaps —'

Red Rosa slammed her bull's pizzle against the side of the stove with a loud thwack. 'Be quiet, you Magyar pig!' she commanded. 'Get out of that bed and come outside with us.'

Von Nagy looked up at her, eyes completely without fear, as if he were resigned to his fate, perhaps even glad that it meant death, now that he had been betrayed thus. 'You are going to kill me, I suppose,' he said quietly. 'Poldi or whoever it is won't want me alive now.' He gave a little sigh and threw back the coarse blankets, revealing that he wore an old-fashioned nightshirt, complete with bed socks.

Ilona giggled at the sight and Red Rosa turned on her angrily. Von Nagy seized his chance. Acting with surprising speed, he made a grab for the automatic that he always kept beneath his pillow, and pressed its muzzle to his temple.

'Look out, Comrade Major!' Vera shrieked.

Red Rosa lashed out with her pizzle. The automatic exploded in the same instant. Von Nagy howled with pain as the slug smashed into his lower jaw, pulping it into a scarlet gory mess through which the shattered bone glittered like polished ivory. The automatic clattered to the floor.

Red Rosa hesitated no longer. There were shouts of alarm from the Hungarians' camp. A whistle shrilled urgently. Someone was running heavily across the snow. 'Shoot him! Finish off the old fool!' she yelled to Vera as von Nagy sagged there on the bunk, moaning softly, the blood jetting from his shattered jaw. '*Fire!*'

Vera flung up her tommy-gun and fired. The racket was tremendous in the close confines of the hut, as she pumped slugs into the desperately writhing and tossing old man on the bed. They ripped the length of his skinny body, gouging huge red holes in his wrinkled old flesh. His hands clawed the air frantically, as if he were attempting to cling on to life itself.

Grinning evilly she pointed the muzzle at his groin, where the blood-soaked nightshirt had ridden up to expose his shrunken genitals, and fired one last burst. Then she let the tommy-gun drop. It was over. Von Nagy was dead — and the Hungarian Cavalry Division was theirs!

Colonel Poldi, fat, overdressed and reeking of perfume, stared ashen-faced and nervous at his new masters as they crowded into the mobile Ops room. Outside they were trying to pacify the General's servant, who had attempted to carry away the horribly mutilated body towards the horse-lines. Apparently he wanted to ride with it back to Hungary. 'My General,' he moaned, kneeling there in the snow, swaying back and forth. 'They have taken my General... Oh my General!'

Red Rosa flashed a look at the Hungarians huddled at one end of the tight caravan, and barked in Russian, '*Boshe Moi*! Shut that fool up at once. He gets on my nerves.'

Poldi nodded to an aide and the man went out. There was the sound of slapping and the moans died away into a series of soft sobs.

'All right,' Red Rosa said. 'Now let us look at the situation. Frantek — report.'

Frantek, very military now in the presence of these scared Hungarian officers, snapped to attention and pointed a dirty finger at the map on the wall. 'The Slovakian People's Army will commence its attack on the line of River Ondava at zero eight hundred hours on the morning of December 1st, comrades,' he barked.

Red Rosa sniggered. So it was 'People's Army' and 'comrades' now, was it? These Slovak pigs learned fast. But she kept her peace and let him get on with it.

'It is the intention of our High Command, comrades,' Frantek continued, 'to force bridgeheads at Svidnik and Stropkov. By this means we will prevent the enemy from sending troops across the river to assist the German XXX Corps.' He clicked his heels together and beamed at the nervous Hungarians, who obviously had not yet become accustomed to the fact that their enemies were now their allies.

Red Rosa shot Poldi a look. In spite of the freezing cold, his fat face was dripping with sweat; it looked as if it had just been rubbed with goose-fat. She waited.

'We Hungarians are happy to hear that our Slovakian — er, comrades are prepared to take offensive action soon after the … soon after the…' His words trailed away as he became suddenly conscious of the big brutal woman's eyes upon him. From now onwards, he told himself, the less he said the better — especially on political matters. One day the Gulag was waiting for him anyway, he knew that; he could only attempt to postpone that terrible day as long as possible.

'So you are happy, eh, comrade?' Red Rosa sneered. 'You are happy that your Slovakian comrades are at last going to do some fighting, after five years of sitting on their fat arses?'

Frantek flushed.

'But what are our dear *Hungarian* comrades going to do now in the fight against the fascists, eh?'

Poldi's bottom lip trembled as if he might burst into tears at any moment. 'What *can* I do, comrade?' he quavered, spreading his hands out, palms upwards — like a damned Jewish pedlar, Red Rosa thought scornfully.

'I'll tell you what you can do, Comrade Colonel,' she rapped. 'Our own glorious Red Army will take care of the Fritz infantry in due course. They are not much better than a disorganised rabble from what I have seen of them.' She frowned at the thought. 'The only effective weapon those fascists still possess are those Stukas of theirs. Only this very day they have struck a terrible blow at our own Air Force at Krakov. Without those dive-bombers flying cover and acting as flying artillery, the Fritzes will cave in. Agreed?'

'Agreed, Comrade Major,' Poldi said unhappily.

'Now, according to our information, these damned flyboys will provide cover for the rest of the Fritzes coming through the pass. They are scheduled to land at a field here —' she pointed at the map with her bull's pizzle — 'near Liptovsky.'

In spite of himself Poldi shivered at the sight of that monstrous, brown, animal knout. What kind of a woman was this who carried such an unnatural object as a whip?

'It is estimated that they will land there tomorrow morning as soon as it is light enough.' Red Rosa looked directly at the Hungarian Colonel. 'It will be the task of your cavalry, Colonel Poldi, to have that field surrounded by dawn tomorrow.'

Poldi forced a weak smile. He was not being forced to act directly against his former allies after all. Unlike the Slovak he would not have to betray the Germans in an overt display of treachery. 'I see, Comrade Major. Yes, I should be able to do that.'

'*Horoscho*!'

'I shall issue the necessary orders immediately.' He turned to an aide and whispered something hurriedly in Magyar. The man saluted and went out into the howling snowstorm. His smile broadened. Surely the female monster would be impressed now by his swift military decision-making and efficiency. It seemed so — for now she too was smiling, though her dark eyes did not light up.

Outside there was the clink of harness and stirrups as the 1st Battalion hurried to mount up, carrying their saddlery with them.

'My men are already preparing to mount up and ride away to carry out your orders, Comrade Major,' Poldi announced proudly.

'Excellent, comrade,' Red Rosa said, voice deceptively soft. 'They will be armed, of course?'

'Of course. But why do you ask?'

'Because,' she hissed, her savage face enjoying his discomfiture, 'when those damned Fritzes land tomorrow morning, your men, Colonel Poldi, will slaughter them — every last man! They are SS. They deserve no other fate.' She gave him one last hard look, and his legs seemed to turn to water; her eyes were like an animal's, dark and glittering, devoid of all feeling. 'Not one single Fritz pig must survive. Understand?'

'Understood,' he echoed weakly, reaching for his silk handkerchief and patting his brow with a hand that trembled visibly.

Opposite him Frantek licked suddenly parched lips and said hoarsely, 'It is the new order, comrade … I am afraid we must learn to live with it.'

'Yes, comrade,' Poldi answered weakly. 'You are right, comrade.' He savoured this new use of the old word 'comrade' for a moment, then turned to his chief-of-operations. 'Comrade Major,' he snapped, fully in charge of himself now. 'I want you to take personal charge of the 1st Battalion. You will answer to me for any failure.'

'Yes, Comrade Colonel,' the other officer answered and, after swinging him a stiff salute, went out.

Red Rosa beamed. They were learning, this scum from the Balkans. They were learning, all right. She raised her pizzle in mock salutation. 'Death to the fascist swine, comrades!'

'Death to the fascist swine!' they echoed — and Frantek raised a clenched fist in the communist salute.

Red Rosa grinned. The Red Army was a wonderful teacher; it made instant communists, even out of fascists.

CHAPTER 2

Heavy-footed, shoulders hunched, the long column of refugees toiled by the airmen squatting on their haunches around little fires cooking their evening meal. A dead woman, several months pregnant to judge from her swollen belly, lay squashed in the snow, arms and legs outstretched, as if she were on the Cross itself. No one paid any attention, no one cared. Men, women and children, they tramped doggedly over her body, pressing her ever deeper into the slush.

To the rear, at the entrance to the pass, the heavy guns were thundering and the night sky was rent by scarlet flashes like lethal summer lightning. The Russians obviously knew the XXX Corps was pulling out of Poland into Slovakia. The barrage was the preliminary to the infantry attack to come at dawn — the Russians' favourite time for an offensive.

Hannemann took the sizzling, slightly charred first sausage from the end of the red-hot shovel on which he had been grilling it over the fire and tossed it to Slack-Arse Schmidt. 'There you are, Bello. Be a good doggie and eat it up.'

'Fuck you!' snarled Slack-Arse but he caught the sausage and began to devour it, eagerly, yelping as it burnt his tongue and licking at the grease running down his unshaven chin.

Wearily Hannemann waited until his own sausage was done, taking periodic sips from their last flatman. To his front an oxcart lumbered by, a woman suckling a dead baby to her plump breast, crooning like a lunatic all the while. In the lurid flickering light of the camp fires, with the thundering guns providing an eerie kind of background music, the scene seemed to typify this whole crazy world. A lunatic suckling a dead infant. The world had gone nuts, thought Hannemann grimly.

A few metres away de la Mazière was squatting with his senior officers, roasting and grilling their own sausages, their last. An hour before, just after they had landed, a message from von Prittwitz's Quartermaster had arrived with the rations, stating that this was the last issue. There would be no more sausages, even for the privileged air crews. Now they would have to forage from the land. 'Forage from the fucking land?' Pegleg had exclaimed angrily. 'This is the High Tatras in the middle of winter! What are we expected to find here in these snows — shitting polar bears or something?'

Now they sat there on their haunches around the pitiful flickering fires, the day's victory already forgotten, sunk in a mood of shivering desperation while the long columns of refugees plodded by, not even exchanging good-humoured banter with the troops as of old, too weary, too frightened to do so.

It was the end, de la Mazière told himself. The end of the German Empire in the East. Soon the red flood would swamp the Reich itself and these same terrible scenes would be repeated all over the Homeland. Once they had surged forward, ever victorious; nothing had seemed capable of stopping that tremendous *blitzkrieg*. But the shoe was on the other foot now, for it seemed that nothing could stop the Russians sweeping in from the east.

Karst sat alone, sausage untouched. He was only half listening to the others. The refugees he did not see. The fate of those humble peasants — lured to this remote land by golden promises that had never been fulfilled — meant nothing to him. He was concerned solely with his own fate. The whole front was collapsing, that was certain. He knew that his comrades had achieved a local victory this afternoon, but that meant precious little. It had simply staved off the day of judgement for a little while longer. That was all. If he didn't act soon, he would end up dead, like all these fools around him. Worse; he might end up facing a lingering death of starvation in a Soviet Gulag.

'It's not fair,' he whined to himself. 'I don't want to die yet. There is so much to be done. Why should I die here in this goddam arsehole of the world? For what? What purpose does it serve, if that decrepit fool von Prittwitz saves a handful of broken-down stubble-hoppers, whose morale is broken for good? They will never fight again with any spirit. The first opportunity they are given and they will desert to the decadent Anglo-Americans on the Western Front. But I am a Karst, an officer, a member of the Armed SS, the élite of the élite. We still have something to offer Greater Germany. So why must I die here?'

He stared angrily into the flickering fire, spitting now and again as fresh flakes of snow drifted into the flames, his face hollowed out to a solemn, gaunt death's head by the shadows. He knew now that it was *sauve qui peut*. Later, back in the Reich, no one would ask how he, Baron Karst, was the only one who had managed to escape from the whole of the 1st SS Stuka Wing. The entire Reich was under siege. No one would have time to ask such awkward questions. The enemy was pressing hard on both fronts; the Tommies bombed by night, the Amis by day. Who would concern themselves with his lone fate?

A convoy of wounded started to pass, laden high in little *panje* wagons dragged by game little Polish ponies, the wounded groaning at every bump and pit hole, while the Red Cross nurses walked through the snow at their sides, trying their best to soothe the unfortunate casualties.

De la Mazière rose and walked across to watch the convoy, accompanied by Pegleg. In the flickering light of their fires, they could see how the shattered blood-stained bodies were piled into the little wagons, each followed by an evil wake of blood and faeces; for all the wounded were suffering from dysentery, too. He shook his head. 'My God, Pegleg, it's a complete breakdown, complete!'

'We're all for the funny farm now, sir,' Pegleg answered and the usual bantering tone had vanished from his voice now.

A line of men faltered by, each with one hand on the shoulder of the man in front of him, all with their eyes blindfolded. They were led by a girl in Red Cross uniform who could not have been a day older than eighteen, urging them on with cheerful cries of, 'It's all right, boys, we're nearly there now. All right now ... nearly there...' Her voice died away in the darkness, together with the hesitant shuffle of the blinded soldiers.

The last of the *panje* wagons trundled past. Now the infantry started to slog by, bent like hunchbacks under the heavy load of their packs, gasping and cursing every time they slipped or stumbled in the slick new snow. They did not look up at the watching SS men. Their gaze was fixed either on their feet or on the exit to the pass.

Staring at their ashen, wild-eyed faces in the glowing light of the little camp fires, de la Mazière told himself that only the iron discipline of the German Army kept them from breaking ranks and making a run for it. Panic hovered just below the surface.

An officer passed. He had lost his helmet and he had a blood-stained bandage wrapped around his blond cropped head. 'Deutscherl's Bavarians, sir,' he called out, as if the information was important.

De la Mazière touched his hand to his cap as if in salute and asked quietly, 'How does it look back there, Lieutenant?'

'Shitty, sir, decidedly shitty,' the young Bavarian officer told him cheerfully enough.

De la Mazière listened to the roar of the Soviet guns and noted the evil pink glittering of the exploding shells to the east. 'Are they attacking in strength?'

'Yessir,' the officer answered. Perhaps he, at least, thought that the retreat was an adventure, de la Mazière told himself. How good it was to be so young and so unimaginative. 'There are millions of the Red buggers back there — well, thousands. They know we're off and they're doing their shitting level best to cut us off...' His voice trailed away as he too vanished into the glowing darkness. The long column of beaten infantry plodded on through the snow.

De la Mazière touched Pegleg's arm, and together they turned, walking slowly back to the fires. Now the only sound was the rumble of the enemy guns and the steady shuffle of the Bavarians slogging westwards. While Pegleg limped on into the darkness, de la Mazière paused at the fires and stared around at the faces of his men, peasants and aristocrats, both. He was their 'Old Man', although most of the air-gunners and many of the ground crew were older than himself. He was responsible for their collective fate. He sucked his teeth thoughtfully and then crooked a finger at Sergeant Diercks, who was fussing with his clipboard, steel-rimmed spectacles at the end of his long nose, trying to make out the figures by the flickering light of the campfire, so that he looked for all the world like some fussy clerk in a nineteenth-century countinghouse. 'Papa!' he called.

Diercks creaked across, hands as always gloveless and black with engine oil. 'Sir?'

'Papa, you know we are scheduled to start operating from the field at Liptovsky on the other side of the pass as soon as it's light enough to land there. It's a one-time Czech Army grass field, I'm told, and hasn't been improved by the Luftwaffe much since. Facilities will be limited, I assume.'

'Don't you worry your head about that, sir,' the old crew chief said emphatically. 'Old Papa Diercks'll see everything is all squared away by the time the Wing is due to land tomorrow morning.' He consulted his clipboard. 'Key ground crews to depart zero three hundred hours ... ETA approximately six hundred hours... That will give us about four and a half hours before first light. At this time of year it don't get light till about eight.'

'Papa,' de la Mazière said gently, trying to stop the flow of words, telling himself that the old man never saw anything but planes and the men who served or flew them. 'You know, the whole damned world could disappear and you'd never notice as long as you had your Stukas to play with. Can't you see what's going on here at the pass?'

Papa Diercks looked up at the tall, handsome officer standing there, snowflakes falling sadly around him. 'Oh, I see, sir... Yes, I see that mess all right. But there's nothing I can do about it, so I just get on with my job. Did it like that with young von Richthofen in the Old War, with poor Colonel Greim in Spain, and have been doing it with you, sir, ever since you took over the Wing. Can't let a little thing like a war interfere with the job of getting my birds airborne!' He shook his old head firmly. 'No *sir*!'

De la Mazière laughed although he had never felt less like laughing. 'In three devils' name, Papa, you really are one for the books! Nothing ever rattles you. I swear you'll still be clutching that damned old clipboard in your paws the day they plant you for good.'

'No doubt, sir,' Papa said, suddenly standing on his dignity. 'But there's got to be order. Schnapps is schnapps and duty is duty,' he added, quoting the old military saying.

'Now, Papa, listen,' de la Mazière said patiently. 'I know your convoy has got priority to bump everything else out of the way on your trip through the pass. But do you think this lot is going to take any notice of that?' He indicated the Bavarians slogging stolidly through the snow, now mixed up with a jam of wretched, cursing civilians. 'You'll have to wait your turn with the rest. This is not simply another withdrawal, Papa, this is a damned retreat — which could well turn into a downright total rout tonight.'

'I'll take my chance, sir,' Papa replied doughtily.

De la Mazière bit his bottom lip with worry. There was no certainty that Papa and his crews would reach the new field by dawn, and without those crews his Stukas would be virtually useless. There was no doubt that the Popovs would bring in new planes by the morrow. What would happen if his Stukas were caught on the ground without sufficient fuel and not properly armed? The answer was obvious. The Popovs would slaughter them...

'Colonel.' Karst's harsh, arrogant voice broke into his thoughts. He spun round.

Karst was standing there, his black jacket powdered with snow, the bright black and silver of the Knight's Cross at his throat, his face set but blank of emotion, as if the misery trudging by only metres away did not exist. Later de la Mazière would realise that at that moment Karst had blotted out everything else but his own damned salvation — but that would be later. 'Yes?' he asked.

'Sir, I have an idea. Sergeant Diercks here only needs a few skilled tradesmen to get the field organised for our arrival — find the local source of fuel, prepare what ammo may be available, etcetera.'

De la Mazière nodded and waited.

'Well, sir,' Karst said glibly, 'I know a way of transporting those key people to the new field in a matter of, say, thirty minutes.'

'How?' de la Mazière said eagerly.

'Fly them in, sir.'

'In *this* weather? Landing at night, and with no flare path?'

'Oh, not the greenbeaks, of course, but people like me, sir, and the retreads, Perspex and Pegleg. If we left our gunners behind we could load three ground crew apiece. Under Sergeant Diercks, those first people could get things started. We'd have fuel for another trip, too, perhaps even three trips before we'd need more juice. With a bit of luck, we could fly in the basic ground staff, while the rest came up by truck. What do you think, sir?' he concluded, lowering his head so that de la Mazière did not see the almost desperate look of longing in his dark eyes.

De la Mazière considered for a moment. They had done it before, of course, right at the start of the great attack on Russia, flying in ground crews to advance fields while the Wehrmacht drove ever deeper into that accursed country. But that had been in the summer of 1941 when there had been only a couple of hours of darkness a day and there had not been snow on the runways. All the same, he knew what a fine pilot Karst was, as were Pegleg and Perspex. That was why they had survived so long. He made his decision. 'Do you think you can really do it, Karst, without wrecking your crate?'

'Of course, sir. With one hand tied behind my back!' Karst replied with a sudden enthusiasm that de la Mazière had never seen before in the sombre Baron. It should have made him suspicious there and then.

De la Mazière hesitated no longer. 'All right, Karst,' he said, then turned to the old crew chief. 'Get on the stick, Papa, and pick up your key men. I'll alert the pilots. All right now, let's move it — *dalli, dalli*.'

Karst's heart leapt madly. He had done it. He was out!

CHAPTER 3

It was still half-dark and a few remaining stars twinkled in the glacial dawn air. A freezing wind blew down the pass straight from Siberia. The last of the ground crews had departed in their trucks, leaving the engines of the remaining Stukas idling over, and had been swallowed up in the mass of the retreat. Now the handful of greenbeaks stood on guard beside their planes, drawn pistols in their hands, while the gunners squatted behind their weapons, pointing them in the direction from which the Russians would come once the last of the Hungarian cavalry had passed through. But where were the damned Hungarians? And where were Karst and two retreads, too? It was nearly three hours since they had departed with Papa Diercks and the others. They should have been back for more ground crew ages ago.

Time and again, de la Mazière flashed an expectant look to the west, but the sky remained obstinately empty of those familiar gull-winged shapes. He clenched his fists, angry with himself for having let Karst talk him into the crazy scheme. Had he lost three planes and twelve good men thanks to Karst? He hoped that he was wrong; he hoped that there had been some kind of hitch at the other end which had prevented them taking off again. Anything, he told himself, could have happened on a night like this.

The infantry coming through the pass were thinning out now, and their pace was quickening as they came past in bunches of fours and fives. There were fewer officers and noncoms amongst them, too, though de la Mazière would have expected there to be more senior men bringing up the rear.

The roar of the Soviet artillery was becoming louder by the minute. Soon they would have to take off, before it was too late. He nodded to Slack-Arse Schmidt, Pegleg's gunner. 'Mount up. You'll have to squeeze in with Hannemann this morning, Sergeant.'

'Hope he's got rid of them shits of his,' Slack-Arse remarked sourly. 'When he lets rip with that fart-cannon of his, sir, he doesn't half make green smoke.' But the gunner nipped up into the plane hurriedly enough — and de la Mazière knew why. They were all becoming very jittery this dawn. He waved his right arm to indicate that his pilots should get in their planes. Cradling his machine pistol in his arms, he watched as they swung themselves up into their cockpits.

The familiar snap-and-crackle of small arms fire echoed further up the pass, and he could see the scarlet stab and flash of Soviet tommy-gun fire up there. The Popovs were getting very close. But still there was no sign of the Hungarian cavalry supposedly protecting the rear.

All around him, the Stukas' engines started to sing ever louder as the pilots revved them up prior to take-off. The prop wash lashed his greatcoat around his legs as he stood there, weapon at the ready.

Now the stubble-hoppers were beginning to run; he saw them stumbling towards him, already throwing away their packs and helmets in panic. It wouldn't be long before their weapons followed. Deutscherl's Bavarians were breaking.

'Better get in, sir!' Hannemann bellowed above the racket. 'There's a Popov T-34 up there — I can see it from here!'

A white-faced officer, blood trickling down the side of his face, lurched towards de la Mazière. Instinctively he shot out one arm to grab the man, forcing him to stop. Tracer was scything the ranks of the running Bavarians now. Men were falling on all sides. Here and there lone soldiers went to ground, waiting for the inevitable. They'd surrender, once the first wave of Popovs had rolled by. 'What's going on?' he bellowed.

'The shitting Hungarians — they've mutinied!' the officer cried in a thick Munich accent, gesturing at the wound on his forehead. 'One shit gave me this with his sabre. Treachery ... treachery on all sides!' He dragged himself free and stumbled on, his eyes rolling wildly, as if the Devil himself were after him.

De la Mazière's heart sank. So that was it. The whole front was collapsing. There was no hope for von Prittwitz's Corps now, especially if the Hungarians in the van had mutinied too.

'Beat it, sir — quick!' Hannemann shrieked urgently, as the first tremendous blast of a tank cannon ripped the dawn air apart. 'There are three of the shits barrelling this way... *Los, los!*'

De la Mazière sprang up onto the wing and slipped behind the controls. A shell howled towards him, like an express train thundering through a station. It exploded to the Stuka's immediate front in a blast of red flame. The Stuka trembled violently, and de la Mazière had to steady himself on his seat as he made his last frantic check. He pressed the R/T button. 'All right, let's hoof it before it's too late! Over and out.'

Behind him Hanneman pressed the trigger. His machine gun spurted fire at the squat shapes in the earth-brown uniform of the Red Army who were coming out of the dawn gloom, firing and yelling that spine-chilling 'Urrah!' of theirs.

The Stukas began to roll forward, jolting and bumping over the uneven snow field. De la Mazière flashed a look to right and left. His greenbeaks were doing well; they were not letting themselves be panicked by this enforced take-off.

A T-34 came rattling in from the right, cannon thundering, machine gun spitting fire — impossible to hit with the Stuka's 37mm while the Stuka was still on the ground. But Hannemann and his fellow gunners, veterans to a man, were equal to the situation. They concentrated a hail of white tracer on the tank. It seemed to be racing through a solid wall of fire, the slugs bouncing harmlessly off its thick steel hide. But the mini-barrage had the desired effect. The driver became rattled, and swung the tank to the left. Its track caught in some sort of drainage ditch and it went keeling over on its side, the track racing round and round like the legs of some helpless, upturned beetle.

Then they were airborne. Rapidly the noise of the fire-fight and the stab and thrust of flame diminished below. They had managed to take off, but a very worried de la Mazière, busy with his green-glowing instruments, had an awful sinking feeling at the thought of what might be waiting for them on landing…

Pegleg groaned. His crotch felt warm and sticky with blood, and he knew he was dying. This time there would be no one to save him. He had reasoned by now, from the horses, that it was the damned Magyars who had attacked them so treacherously.

At first they had circled the field, dropping flares in order to get some idea of what the situation was. Then, guided by the swinging lanterns of the Hungarian cavalrymen, they had come in to land.

It had been nip and tuck. Twice he was forced to pull back the stick and take to the air again; but finally, blessedly, the wheels had hit the wet tarmac and he had been running straight and true — right into the Hungarians' machine-gun fire.

Pegleg's canopy had shattered, and behind him he'd heard old Papa Diercks' shrill scream as the burst ripped his face away, his features dripping down onto his chest like molten red wax. Blinded, Pegleg had careened forward. He had felt the plane bouncing off the tarmac. Undercarriage shattered, the Stuka had gone flying over the snow on its belly, metal rending and screeching, great chunks of it flying off, until suddenly there had been an awesome crash. Pegleg had been flung violently forward, hitting his head against the instrument panel, and he had blacked out.

When he'd come to, he found himself suspended upside down in his straps, his head whirling, eyes staring in blank incomprehension at the shattered faces of his dead companions.

It had taken him a long time to recognise what the persistent hissing was — gas, dripping from his carburettors onto the red-hot engine! That had galvanised him into desperate activity, struggling valiantly with the straps that held him suspended thus, head a few millimetres away from the rudder bar. Somehow he had managed to get upright. His tin leg had gone, perhaps wrenched off in the crash, and as he finally managed to undo the straps and fell helplessly to the snow, he had heard the squelch of the clogged blood at the base of his stomach. Then the pain had hit him...

For a long moment he'd lain there dazed, head feeling as if someone were thrusting a metal skewer through it. Still there was that hiss of escaping gas. He had to get away. But why? To save his own life? *No*, to warn the others about what was waiting for them here.

He had begun to crawl away from the wrecked plane, leaving a blood-red trail on the snow behind him. Further off he'd seen a mounted patrol — Hungarians, armed with lances, of all things, glinting in the dirty white light of the new dawn. He had got as far as a clump of stunted bushes and collapsed there, sobbing for breath, feeling himself weaken by the moment. How could he warn the others? *How?*

Then he had it. '*Shit-house paper*, old friend — that's the way to do it… Good old shit-house paper…' Suddenly, even as his life blood ebbed away, he smiled. With fingers that felt like clumsy sausages, he started to fumble inside his tunic.

Karst's engine began to splutter and thump alarmingly. Just as he had planned… He frowned, fiddling with the controls as his three ground crew crouched in the cockpit looked at him in alarm. 'Don't worry,' he told them, 'everything is all right, even if the crate's acting up. In five minutes we should be over our lines.' He pretended to be adjusting his instruments as the Stuka started to lose height, bucking and jerking all over the pre-dawn sky.

Karst was feeling pleased with himself. Everything was going exactly as he had planned. He had waited till Pegleg and Perspex had gone in to land in the darkness below, watching unsurprised as their touch-down was greeted by a burst of machine-gun fire. Perhaps, he reasoned, the Popov partisans had infiltrated the field. Perhaps it was the Slovaks. He didn't know and he didn't care. But the firing had provided him with the perfect excuse.

'Trouble down there, men!' he had snapped, increasing speed at once and starting a rapid climb. 'Can't risk it. Must find a field somewhere else.'

There were no protests from the frightened ground crew, who had never flown before. They accepted his decision tamely.

Now he wanted rid of them. In the first red glint of the new day he could see the silver shimmer of a river, the River Ondava, which marked the boundary of Eastern Slovakia. Beyond that river was safety. It was time to ditch the only witnesses of his defection. He let the plane go into a sudden dive. Next to him, the little corporal with the terrible breath heaved, face turned green.

'What's up, sir?' he gasped, hand to his mouth as if he might vomit at any moment.

Karst played the cool hero. 'Nothing to worry about. That firing might have hit a fuel line. Better to be prepared, though. Take my parachute.'

'Your parachute, sir?' the man quavered.

'Don't worry, man. It'll be all right. But you'd better…' He did not end his sentence. Instead he pressed his throat-mike and commanded: 'Trouble with the engine. Sure we can make it. All the same, you two had better buckle on the chutes. If anything goes seriously wrong, I'll give you a signal well in time. Over and out.'

The ashen-faced crewmen fumbled feverishly with the unfamiliar buckles and straps, struggling into the parachute harnesses in the tight confines of the cockpit.

Karst smiled to himself, eyes filled with triumph. It was working. *It was working*! He was getting out of that damned wandering goose-egg before it was too late. He let the plane drift a bit lower.

There was some kind of trouble going on down there. He could see the grey smoke of gunfire, stabbed here and there by flame, rolling across the river. But he could just make out, too, the huge silken swastikas spread out over the snow, and the blood red flag of Nazi Germany. Those were German positions — he was almost there!

'Men,' he cried, 'you'll have to bale out!' The engine stuttered alarmingly. 'I can't hold her much longer! Jettisoning canopy … *now!*' The cockpit cover flew away and the icy wind buffeted him across the face. He barely noticed. He was going to get rid of these unwanted witnesses: that was all that concerned him.

Down below dark figures were streaming towards the river, carrying what looked like assault boats. But it seemed that the German fire was aimed at their ranks, for men were stumbling and falling everywhere.

'This is the drill. In exactly ten seconds I shall do the loop. Got that? Ten seconds. Release your hold and let yourselves be thrown out. Count three — *slowly*, do you hear? — and then pull the rip-cord… All right, here we go!' Gently he turned the plane over on its back, held in himself by his seat straps. '*Let go!*' he roared above the rushing wind.

Two of them immediately did as commanded. It was as if an invisible hand had suddenly snatched them, plucking them from the safety of the cockpit and flinging them to the earth far below. Eyes gleaming in triumph behind his goggles, Karst counted with them — 'One … two … three…' — as they hurtled towards the ground, turning over and over like star divers performing somersaults before an admiring crowd. A flash of white, a stream of shroud lines, and the first man's parachute had blossomed into a silken white flower. A moment later the second man's chute opened up too; that tremendous fall was braked and the two ground crew men were floating gently downwards — straight, Karst hoped, into the arms of the enemy!

But the third man, the corporal with the terrible breath, clung on there with white-knuckled hands, blond thatch falling over his green-tinged face, eyes bulging with terror. 'I can't do it, sir!' he yelled. 'I just *can't!* I'm shit scared…'

'Get out, man!' Karst cried furiously as they hung there upside down and the first glowing balls of flak shells began to hurtle up towards the Stuka like a chain of fiery pearls. 'Go on — *move*!'

Still the corporal clung on desperately.

Karst lost his temper. Gripping the stick between his knees, he pulled out his pistol and pointed it at the corporal. 'Go on — out!'

But it seemed the man was too terrified even to understand the threat.

A shell exploded near the Stuka, sending it reeling and yawing through the sky. Karst felt a thrill of fear. 'My God,' he cried, 'we're sitting ducks up here! *Get out*!' He slammed the muzzle of his pistol across the corporal's white knuckles still clinging onto the side of the cockpit.

The man screamed hysterically and let go. Next moment he was sailing out of the cockpit, a confused, panicked bundle of flailing arms and legs.

Karst acted at once. He pulled back the stick frantically. The Stuka roared straight upwards, leaving the floating grey puffballs of the flak behind rapidly. Down below the corporal fell and fell. He did not open his parachute. Then he was gone — and Karst was crossing the silver snake of the River Ondava, racing towards safety.

'Now my shitting flipper's gone over to the shitting enemy!' Pegleg cursed as his left hand suddenly gave way beneath him and he fell helplessly into the snow, gasping for breath. He was crawling back towards his crashed Stuka now. It was only twenty metres away, but to him it seemed like twenty kilometres. He lay there, feeling as weak as a baby, the only sound the faint clatter of the Hungarian cavalry and persistent hiss of the escaping gas from the plane's carburettors.

To left and right of the old runway, just in front of the second wrecked Stuka — which had to be either Perspex's or Karst's — the dismounted Hungarians were digging in their evil-looking machine guns, ugly snouts tilted towards the dawn sky.

It seemed to take the dying man lying there in a patch of blood-stained snow a long time to comprehend why. Then he understood at last. Of course — they were going to slaughter the rest of the Wing when they attempted to land! The 1st SS were flying right into a trap. He shook his head and everything swung back into focus.

'Pegleg, you silly old fart,' he croaked weakly to himself, 'the friendly fellows in white coats will be coming for you soon … if you go on like this…' He coughed painfully, and a thick jelly-like gob of black blood edged its way out of the side of his gaping mouth. 'Rubber van … and funny farm,' he gasped weakly and spat it out onto the snow, only millimetres away from his nose. 'Got to get on with it… Come on, flipper, back old Pegleg up.'

With an effort of sheer naked willpower, he levered himself up; this time his arm didn't give. 'Thanks, flipper,' he breathed fervently and crawled on, ears already aware of the first faint hum of a distant aeroplane. Next to the line of massed machine guns, orders were being barked and gunners were flinging themselves into position for the slaughter to come.

Now he was only metres away from the upturned Stuka, gasping and wheezing, fighting off the black waves which threatened to swamp him for good. He had always known it would end like this. 'Paying the butcher's bill now,' he croaked, something akin to madness in his dying eyes now. 'All the medals, all the girls in black stockings, the parties … the glory.'

Again he spat out a gobbet of blood. The roar of engines was getting ever closer. 'Must ... hurry,' he choked. 'Must ... hurry...'

The wrecked Stuka loomed up, stark and black in front of him, seeming to fill the whole horizon. He reached up one hand, the other clutching the roll of lavatory paper. Twice he failed to gain a hold on the shattered fuselage and fell gasping and sobbing back into the snow, his strength ebbing away rapidly, bright red lights exploding in front of his eyes. Then he did it. He hung there on the engine, sobbing for breath, fighting off the black eagle of death, which threatened to snatch him away at any moment.

Hanging there, he somehow managed to unscrew the filler cap with his other hand. What he intended was standing operating procedure when a pilot was down in enemy territory. It was based on an edict from 'Fat Hermann' himself. No German plane should ever fall into the hands of the enemy intact; it was an offence punishable by death. So every pilot had taken to carrying a roll of toilet paper with him when flying into action, invariably quipping: 'Just in case I get caught short!' But it was not intended for that purpose; it was to be inserted in the open fuel tank of a ditched plane, rolled out and ignited at a safe distance by the pilot to set the aircraft afire.

Pegleg knew he would never reach a safe distance now. It didn't matter anyway. He was dying. He knew it. Now he inserted the end of the pink roll into the tank and hung on there, sobbing with the effort, blood streaming afresh from his terrible wounds.

The noise of the planes was overpowering now. They were about to land. Feebly he fumbled with his presentation lighter — a silver one, given to him back in the good old days by no less a person than Reichsführer SS Himmler himself, '*On the occasion of the award of the Knight's Cross*', as the inscription read. He laughed weakly at the memory and flicked the flint-wheel. Nothing happened.

At their machine gun posts the Hungarian officers were rapping out orders, while their horses whinnied nervously behind them, rearing up and trying to break their hobbles. Now the noise of what was left of the 1st SS Stuka was ear-splitting. Desperately Pegleg tried again. Dying as he was, he could tell by the sound of the engines that they were coming in to land. 'God, I've *got* to do it!' he cried in sudden despair and flipped the wheel of the lighter once again. A flutter of blue sparks. Nothing. A burning sense of frustration. It was going to be too late, too late … the flame! *The blessed flame*! He could just make it out, wavering in the mist that was threatening to engulf him. 'Funny farm … rubber van…' He let the lighter drop. It hit the fuel-soaked roll of pink paper. *Whoosh*! As he died, Pegleg heard the roar of the fuel igniting, and he smiled as he sank to the ground, eyes closed at last. 'Friendly fellows in white…' he whispered, not even feeling the heat as the all-consuming flames embraced him.

CHAPTER 4

'Hello, Control ... hello, Control, do you read me?... Control, do you read me — *please*?' Desperately de la Mazière tried to raise the square concrete tower below. But in vain. Control, if there was anyone down there in the first place, was refusing to answer. Nor were there any landing lights, the familiar flares hissing into the dawn sky, the urgent bustle of crewmen running out of the cluster of huts to meet the landing planes. There was something wrong, de la Mazière knew it. There had been something wrong right from the start. What *had* happened to Karst and the retreads?

'Sir!' a panicked young voice crackled urgently over the R/T. It was the greenbeak to his port, his face an anxious white blur behind his canopy. 'I'm out of juice. Can we land, sir? *Over!*' The request ended on a near-scream.

De la Mazière flashed a look at his instrument panel. His own fuel tank was nearly empty, with the red warning light flickering on and off. 'All right — permission to land. Johann One to all, permission to land.' He gasped suddenly. Down to the right of the runway, a Stuka lay sprawled, black against the snow like a shattered crow, a dark figure hanging half out of the wrecked canopy. It was Perspex, he knew it instinctively. Next moment he glimpsed Perspex's personal emblem: a highly stylised pair of bright red silk knickers flamboyantly painted next to the cowling. '*Johann One to all!*' he cried frantically. 'Watch out —'

His engine gave a sudden alarming stutter. His instrument panel flickered red and green. He was in trouble, big trouble. The stick was shuddering violently in his grasp. There was nothing left for him but to go down now. They were all going down — straight into the twin line of machine-gunners already swinging their weapons to meet the gull-winged invaders. De la Mazière swallowed hard. What in three devils' name was going on down there?

Now they were coming down rapidly in two groups of four, while those twin lines of guns swung round inexorably to meet them. Sweat started to trickle down the small of de la Mazière's back. Something was very wrong. But there was not a thing he could do about it. His vest stuck to his skin like a damp towel.

A continuous stream of sparks, red and angry, escaped from his radiator. His engine stuttered and belched obscenely. He took a big gulp of air and prepared for what must come. His hand shook as he reduced throttle. His flaps were down, prop set at fine pitch. He was going into his approach.

Abruptly it happened. A thunderclap of fire. Both sides of the runway burst into flames. Tracer hissed towards them like a glowing white wall. To their front there was a huge flash of flame as one of the Stukas burst apart; its gas tank had exploded.

The first flight of four hit the tarmac. Throttling back madly, they ran straight to their destruction. The inexperienced greenbeaks didn't have a chance. It wasn't war, it was a massacre. Obediently, they let themselves be slaughtered as they fought the landing.

At that range the Hungarians could not miss. Planes were ripped, shredded to metallic skeletons, before they had skidded to a halt. The pilot dead at the controls, a Stuka slammed right into the control tower. Its nose crumpled like a banana skin. None of the others got out. Another plane, its undercarriage shot away, skimmed across the runway like a water bug over the surface of a lake, violent sparks erupting from its ruptured belly. Both wings fell off. It sailed on. A Hungarian machine-gun crew in its path scattered madly. Nothing seemed to stop that metallic torso. But it could not escape the dread fate of the 1st SS Stuka Wing this terrible dawn. Suddenly it furrowed into a little group of wooden huts. Planks flew in every direction. A terrific, blinding flash of light. The engine, severed from the fuselage, rose high into the air, a whirling of flame and blazing fragments.

'Take off!... *TAKE OFF AGAIN!*' de la Mazière shrieked hysterically as his own flight hit the deck, Hannemann's machine gun blazing left and right, spewing death at the treacherous Hungarians.

Too late the greenbeaks, paralysed by shock, rolled to their death, as their predecessors had done.

Bang ... bang ... bang! Tracer flashed across in front of de la Mazière's nose, a blaze of flying death. For a second he froze to the marrow of his bones, unable to react, accepting his fate like a dumb animal, as his Stukas blazed and crashed on all sides, littering the tarmac with their blazing carcasses. Suddenly the instinct of self-preservation returned. He hit the rudder and jerked the stick back. The plane began to climb — but not for long. Now he too was flying at 150 kmh into that blazing inferno, the death pyre of the 1st SS Stuka, tracer zipping towards him in lethal fury from all sides.

There was a sudden burning slap across his face. He almost blacked out. His eardrums were pierced by the shriek of the wind. His canopy had been holed in half a dozen places. He narrowed his eyes, shaking his head, trying to make sense out of this horrific moment. It seemed to take him a long time to become aware of Hannemann's voice screaming in his earphones. What was he saying?

'The shitting undercarriage has gone!... Undercarriage gone!... GONE!'

Next to him another of his Stukas exploded like a grenade. A blinding flash. A black, oily cloud. His plane was surrounded by whirling, gleaming metallic debris. An engine rolled along the ground below like a ball of fire.

Clusters of luminous balls of tracer ricocheted off the tarmac only metres below him, striking up vicious angry sparks. He swerved violently to left and right, but that massed fire followed the crippled Stuka relentlessly.

Now he was the last survivor. The Stukas burned on all sides. Somehow he managed to fly on, smoke pouring from his crippled engine, the fuselage shredded and trailing shattered metal. Noxious glycol fumes were pouring into the cockpit. 'Canopy off,' he commanded. 'Hurry — canopy off!' It disappeared with a rush. Cold air drove away the fumes.

The field raced by at a tremendous rate. They were less than ten metres off the deck, followed still by that awesome weight of flying metal. The series of unlit lamps marking the edge of the airfield shot past. A blinding triangle of light rushed up to meet the crippled plane. De la Mazière closed his eyes instinctively, like a terrified child. Next instant the Stuka hit the ground with an appalling bang.

The propeller blades broke off. The engine churned into the ground, sending mud and snow flying upwards. The cannon dug into the earth and was bent as if it were made of tin. Suddenly the Stuka had come to rest.

The shock hurtled de la Mazière forward towards the instrument panel. His straps caught him in time. He gasped with pain as they cut into his flesh. He felt the slap of the stick against his kneecap and gasped again. Wires snapped everywhere. The tail plane fell off. He felt a searing pain in his side.

Carried away by that terrific momentum, the wrecked Stuka stood on its nose. For one long agonising moment, they were suspended in space. Up front, de la Mazière hung on desperately, one foot jammed against the instrument panel, the snowy plain standing before his eyes like a white wall. Would the crippled Stuka tip over on its back?

It slammed down the next instant, right on its belly. The straps gave him one last vicious bite. Then silence, an ear-piercing, loud-echoing silence, through which a mesmerised de la Mazière could hear the hiss of escaping glycol and fuel vaporising against the hot metal of the engine.

Suddenly he became aware of their danger. He screwed himself round with difficulty. Hannemann and Slack-Arse gawped at him stupidly. Slack-Arse was bleeding from a deep gash in his forehead, but they were both alive, thank God. He freed himself from his straps. '*Los*,' he cried. 'OUT ... OUT ... OUT!'

He grabbed Hannemann by the hair and yanked hard. That did it.

Hannemann howled with pain and cried, 'Get yer frigging hands off — *sir*! My wig's coming off!'

'If those frigging Hungarians get you, Hannemann, more than your wig'll come off! Come on — let's make steam!'

Moments later they were tumbling out of the wrecked plane, running furiously for the cover of a stand of fir trees, while behind them they could hear the fast approaching rumble of horses' hooves. The Hungarians were giving chase.

All around them on that shattered field of death, the Stukas of the 1st SS burned steadily. The slaughter was over. They had fought their last battle in the East. And lost.

Red Rosa walked among the dead and dying Germans spread out in a long line along one side of the field, watched in silence by the Hungarians. To her right, the Stukas continued to burn.

Colonel Poldi and Major Frantek followed the huge woman, saying nothing, eyes full of horror at the state of these young German officers, once their friends, now their foes.

The Russian woman paused in front of a dead German, his arms stretched out stiffly like those of a scarecrow, his face a charred horror out of which peeped two suppurating purple holes that had once contained eyes. She stared down calmly, totally unmoved by that terrible sight, then bent and prodded the corpse with her monstrous knout. It heaved surprisingly and gave a long, low groan. It was the gas within the body escaping.

Poldi gasped with shock and Frantek flashed his hand to his mouth as if he were going to be sick.

Red Rosa did not seem to notice it. 'The Fritz as I like to see him,' she announced calmly. 'On his knees — dead.' She stirred the thing again and it turned over slowly and dramatically, gasping the whole while.

Poldi fought with himself to prevent himself from drawing his sabre and cleaving this female monster from head to toe with it. At his side Frantek felt the small hairs at the back of his head stand erect with fear. How terrible it was to be a member of a small nation standing in the path of the giants, he told himself once again. Always one was humiliated by these pigs.

The huge woman noticed neither Poldi's anger nor Frantek's resentment. Their days were numbered, once they had served their purpose of ensuring that their countries were taken over by the Red Army. She turned away from the dead fascists. To her front the horizon flickered an ominous, silent pink. That was where the Slovaks were fighting the Fritzes on the river. In between lay a great stretch of no-man's-land, in which the survivors of the Fritzes' XXX Corps fought their way desperately westwards to the river. It would be a great slaughter-ground.

There was no more time to be wasted. Already the first Cossack cavalry were streaming out of the pass in a charge, their sabres glittering silver in the sun, their hoarse voices raised in a mighty bass chorus as they chanted over and over again: *'Krasnaya Armya!... Long live the Red Army!...'*

Her savage heart swelled with pride. The forces of the Soviet Motherland, which had suffered so much at the hands of the Fritzes and their jackals — the Rumanians, Slovaks, Hungarians, Italians and all the rest of the pack — were triumphant at last. Now it was the turn of the Fritzes to learn what suffering was.

'*Davai!*' she cried imperiously, slapping her bull's pizzle against her boot. 'There is no more time to be wasted. None of the fascists must escape to the river. It will be a great slaughter...' She strode away towards the waiting horses, with the other two following her helplessly.

Behind them on the field, the body of Major von Kramm, once known as 'Pegleg', stiffened in the dawn cold, arms outstretched like some black Jesus on the Cross...

CHAPTER 5

Now von Prittwitz's 'goose-egg' was finally broken. His XXX Corps was in full flight out of the mountains and across the snow-bound wastes of Eastern Slovakia. Here and there, battalions managed to stick together as recognisable military formations, but they were in the minority. Now field-greys were mingled everywhere with the pathetic columns of fleeing civilians, fighting desperately against Slovak regulars and partisans, Hungarian cavalry and marauding bands of Red Army Cossacks, frantically trying to reach the river before death overtook them.

On the second day of the flight, they took General Gross of the 10th. They stripped him naked, the Slovak partisans jeering coarsely at the shrunken genitals hanging below his enormous bloated belly; then they nailed him to a barn door, arms outstretched, in a sadistic parody of the Crucifixion. But Gross did not make a good Jesus. In death his face was not sad and composed; no saintly look of compassion warmed the gentle eyes. He was a tortured Christ, with crazed bulging eyes, his throat cut from ear to ear in a great ragged, dripping line. And his penis had been sliced off.

Deutscherl was trapped in another barn with a handful of his mountain boys. There was no surrender for the Bavarians. They fought off the Hungarians to the very last. When their ammunition finally gave out, they shot each other with their last slug. Deutscherl calmly blew away the side of his head, in full view of the awed Hungarian cavalry, face set in a look of icy contempt. The Hungarians slunk away back into the forests from whence they had come, with not even the heart to loot the bodies of their former allies.

Von Prittwitz and a handful of his staff officers were overrun by a Cossack patrol, caught out in the open in the middle of snow-bound pastures. The Cossacks charged with their usual drunken, reckless bravado, swinging their silver sabres, slipping down the sides of their mounts, as von Prittwitz's young officers formed a defensive circle around their aged chief and opened fire.

They didn't have a chance. Within five minutes, most of them were dead or dying, and the triumphant wild riders in their black frock coats and rakishly tilted hats set about the task of slitting the survivors' throats and looting the bodies. Just in time the Sotnik in charge realised he had captured a Fritz corps commander and prevented his men from killing von Prittwitz.

That evening Red Rosa personally flogged the old man to death with that monstrous knout of hers. Not even towards the end, when the naked general was forced on to his skinny knees, his broken nose jetting blood, his left eye ripped out, one arm hanging limp and broken at his side, did he utter one plea, one cry, even a moan of pain. He died with his swollen lips tightly closed, not one sound escaping from them right to the very end. Later that evening Red Rosa took Ilona savagely and cruelly, and had her sobbing with pain within minutes.

The retreat went on. On all sides the half-starved, desperate field-greys were attacked by the combined forces of their new enemies. Time and time again their ranks were stormed and thinned by the red tide. Time and time again the survivors pulled back, their sense of betrayal growing ever greater. Now neither side was taking prisoners. No quarter was given or expected.

They passed through that vast empty landscape like a trail of insignificant ants, their path marked by the tell-tale looted bodies of the dead. The very countryside breathed hostility. Those who still had the strength to do so, looked over their shoulders constantly, half-expecting to see those fur-capped monsters on horseback slipping out of the woods to begin the day's slaughter. Others concentrated solely and totally on keeping moving. The wind now spread an icy layer over everything — carts, trucks, cannon, bodies. Men wept with the agony of that cold. Icicles hung from their nostrils. Their beards and eyebrows glittered white with hoar-frost. Every new breath was like a knife-stab to the lungs. To touch the metal of their weapons or vehicles was to touch a red-hot poker. The flesh was ripped from their fingers instantly, revealing the bright white bone beneath. Soldiers, the tears frozen to their ashen cheeks like icy pearls, simply closed their eyes, sank to their knees in the snow and let themselves die. Others took another way out. There were mutual suicide pacts. On the command three, two utterly exhausted and defeated field-greys would blow each other's brains out. Some, without friends, wedged their own rifles against their temples, thrust a big toe through the trigger guard and ended their misery thus. Now carts with the civilians were piled high with the dead, so that they looked as if they were carrying heaps of logs.

On the third day of the great retreat to the river, the Russian Yaks took to the air again. Diving out of the bright hard ball of the winter sun, they hit the straggling convoys of civilians and soldiers, with their guns chattering madly. They had a field day. They couldn't miss — and there was no defence. The refugees were too weary even to flee. Hedgehopping, engines screaming all-out, ugly violet lights rippling the length of their wings, they shot up convoy after convoy, to go racing into the merciless sky, whirling round in loops of triumph, leaving behind them fresh columns of smoke mushrooming to the heavens, exploding tracer zig-zagging crazily in every direction, wounded, riderless horses stampeding madly across that limitless snow plain — and the new dead, soldiers and civilians, men, women and children. Again the survivors trudged on. The flight continued.

On the fourth day, those in the van could see the flickering of the permanent barrage to their front. They were approaching the river. Their pace quickened. They streamed across the newly devastated land towards that angry growling, an ominous wall of sound, which presented a new danger and threatened to engulf them. But they were driven on by the crazy fantasy that somehow they would manage to get through the Slovak lines and cross the river to their own people — and safety. They were plagued with strange illusions. Reach the next wood … that stone wall … the shattered barn to the left … and they would do it. It was a sign: a sign that they were going to make it across the river. Like sleepwalkers, seeing nothing but the wood, the wall, the barn, they stumbled on, eyes filled with almost unbearable longing, towards the flickering cherry-red lights in the grey gloom that was the front…

Right from the start, the three of them had cut themselves off from the rest of the great retreat. 'Sacrificial lambs, doomed for slaughter,' de la Mazière had declared. 'Come on — let's leave the main road and tracks.' Without even waiting to see if the two noncoms were following him, he had left the road and plunged into the snowy fields.

The days had passed in an eternity of weary marching, lying in ditches, under dripping pines, plodding on again across that endless steppe, numb with fatigue, each man assailed at times by a feeling of unutterable loneliness, timeless unreality, a sense of frozen desolation, when the sound of the falling snow sounded louder than the thunder of the distant guns.

It was only de la Mazière's iron SS willpower that kept the two Luftwaffe noncoms going. He seemed without fatigue. When they sank into mindless inactivity at every break, too weary and numb even to get out of the snow, he would still be on his feet, scouting around for something to eat or lighting a fire to melt the snow, so that at least they had a drink of hot water to sustain them.

More than once, when Hannemann or Slack-Arse felt they could go on no longer, for even Hannemann's gigantic strength was ebbing rapidly, de la Mazière bullied, cajoled, pleaded, threatened — and when threats did not work, he resorted to kicks and blows to get them back on their feet again and moving. Always the tall haggard Colonel seemed to possess just one last reserve of strength.

Once, on the second day when they had had nothing to eat for twenty-four hours, they came across a convoy of ambushed civilians, their vehicles shattered and partially looted, dead women sprawled everywhere among the bloated corpses of the ponies.

Hannemann had vomited, while Slack-Arse, hardened veteran that he was, hid his face in his hands. De la Mazière hadn't hesitated. His face revealing nothing, he had croaked, 'Search them — there might still be some food the Cossacks didn't find... Move it! Sharp now!...'

Reluctantly the two noncoms commenced the ghastly business of searching the wrecked carts and then the bodies for the life-saving food they might find — and they had found some, in the haversack of one of the drivers, his guts slit open by a Cossack sabre, the viscera swelling out of the hole like a giant grey-green sea anemone.

Hannemann had at first refused to eat the handful of crusts from the haversack that de la Mazière handed him as his share, but de la Mazière had been harsh and brutal in his determination that the big NCO should eat. 'You will swallow that bread!' he had growled, eyes blazing in his emaciated face, hand falling to his pistol. 'Otherwise I will shoot you, Hannemann, have no doubt of that. I will shoot you in cold blood for disobeying an order!'

And the Colonel had meant what he said, Hannemann knew; there had been no mistaking that killer's look. Feeling as if he must vomit at every bite, he had swallowed the food, trying not to see those sightless eyes all around, staring at him, as if in bitter reproach that he lived and they were dead.

'What's got into the Old Man, Slack?' he had asked his friend afterwards, as the two noncoms squatted in the shelter of one of the carts, while de la Mazière crouched by himself, his eyes blank. 'I've never seen him like this before... Do you think it's the Wing ... or those poor little mites?' He had indicated the dead girls.

Slack-Arse had shrugged wearily. 'Search me, Hannemann. I don't know ... I don't know anything any more.' He had shuddered suddenly. 'But it gives me the creeps to look at him... You know, Hannemann, I think he's ripe for poor old Pegleg's funny farm now...'

By the fourth day, Colonel de la Mazière was swaying wildly like a drunk as he staggered forward over that limitless plain, talking to himself, mumbling and groaning, sometimes waving his hands in the air as if remonstrating with an invisible companion.

Hannemann, about all-in himself, hadn't the strength to follow the Colonel's crazy conversation, but more than once he caught the name 'Karst' and the word 'treachery'. Once de la Mazière stopped in his tracks and Hannemann almost blundered into him, shaking his head as de la Mazière raised his fist at that grey brooding sky and cried, 'By God, Karst, you'll pay for this … I'll find you, if it's last thing I do…' And then the Old Man was staggering on again as if nothing had happened, talking to himself once more.

By the morning of the fifth day he had taken to marching with a drawn pistol in his hand, red-rimmed eyes ablaze with madness, searching the terrain ahead and crying in a cracked hoarse voice, 'Damn you, Karst, damn you!... Where are you?... Be a man and meet your fate… It's no use hiding, I'll find you in the end…'

Behind him a horrified Hannemann whispered to his companion, 'He's flipped, Slack. The Old Man ain't got his cups in his cupboard any more. He's for the funny farm now, Slack…'

And all that a stricken Slack-Arse could do by way of an answer was to nod his head, his gaze fixed on that tall scarecrow in front of him, waving his pistol in the air, cackling crazily to himself as he jerked along in the eerie shuffle of a madman.

That afternoon they saw the river for the first time.

The tanks were rumbling across the snow fields, the dark figures of Slovak infantry moving crouched behind them in tight little groups. From the German side of the river mortars and cannon were firing back. Exploding shells flung whirling pillars of black smoke hurtling up towards the hard blue sky. Here and there the little Skodas were hit, heeling and reeling and sometimes turning over, their broken tracks falling behind them, exposing their infantry to the deadly tracer zipping across the river.

It was, from their vantage point on the wooded height, as if they were watching some UFA newsreel, save that the loud bombastic voice of the commentator was absent.

Behind the two noncoms viewing the scene, de la Mazière slept, grinding his teeth occasionally, whimpering softly now and again, crying out in his sleep or mumbling a few incoherent words, the whole time twitching and turning in the snow as if he were having a terrible nightmare.

Hannemann gritted his teeth desperately and tried to blot out the sounds as he concentrated on the river. 'They're not gonna get across today, Slack-Arse,' he announced. 'Our stubble-hoppers are chopping 'em up for mincemeat nicely.'

'So?'

'So, that means once they've had a noseful and the light goes, they'll dig in on this side of the shitting river for the night.'

Behind them, de la Mazière had settled on his back, lying spreadeagled, his mouth open. He did not seem to be breathing at all. Hannemann could almost have sworn he was dead at that moment, save for the nervous fluttering of his hands. He knew he had to get him over the river and to a doctor soon; he wouldn't last much longer.

'I once knew a whore who worked the Lehrter Station in Berlin,' Slack-Arse mused as Hannemann surveyed the scene below. 'Must have been back in 1935. Anyhow, one day she went home and hammered a nail right through her hat into her turnip. Dead on arrival. She hammered the nail in so good that they had to bury the old women with her bonnet on. Despair, I suppose.'

Hannemann stared at him open-mouthed. 'Are you getting ready for the shitting rubber van as well, Slack-Arse?' he exploded suddenly. 'And what in shit's name was all that supposed to mean?'

'Nothing,' Slack-Arse admitted. 'I was just thinking aloud, Hannemann, that's all.'

'Well, don't!' his running-mate snapped firmly. 'I've got enough shitting trouble on my hands as it is, without you going soft on me as well.'

'I'll be all right, Hannemann,' Slack-Arse said somewhat lamely.

'All right, arse-with-ears. Now, this is what we're gonna do... You see that bunch of shot-up Skodas at three o'clock?'

'Uh ... yes, I see 'em.' Slack-Arse's gaze focused on the charred and twisted Skodas with bright silver holes skewered into their metal hides where armour-piercing shells had penetrated them. Around them was heaped a ghastly tableau of bodies, thrown together in indiscriminate confusion, with one stiff frozen hand poking upwards as if in supplication.

'They reach almost to the river... They'd make the cover we need, Slack-Arse.'

'But we couldn't swim the river, not with the Old Man the way he is, Hannemann,' his running-mate objected.

'We're not gonna swim! In this weather, that water'd block yer outside plumbing in zero-comma-nothing seconds, man! *Mensch*, have you got a little dickie bird that goes twit-twit in yer upper storey?' he added contemptuously.

'Well, how *are* we gonna get across?'

'Simple, plush-ears! Look, the river's already frozen to ice near the banks on both sides. Once night falls and the temperature sinks again, the middle'll be covered with ice too. Of course, our boys on the other side'll be chucking a few mortar shells into the water at regular intervals, to try to prevent it freezing over so that those Slovak shite-heels can't sneak across. But they can't break up the ice everywhere. So let's hope they don't try where we're gonna cross. What do you say, Slack-Arse?'

Slack-Arse did not consider long. 'We ain't got no other alternative, have we, old house?'

Suddenly very sombre, Hannemann shook his head. 'No we ain't, old friend,' he agreed softly. 'If we don't make it tonight —' he flashed a quick look at the sleeping de la Mazière, his breath already beginning to fog again as the temperature started to sink once more — 'we'll lose the Old Man.'

'You mean he'll croak?'

Hannemann hesitated. 'Possible — but that's not what I meant.' He gestured with one dirty forefinger, describing a circle next to his right temple. '*Loopy*,' he said, 'the Old Man'll go completely loopy if we don't get him to a pill-pusher soon...'

It was almost as if de la Mazière was aware that he was being talked about; for suddenly he sat bolt upright, his eyes, however, screwed tightly together. 'Karst,' he announced, his voice taut but perfectly under control, 'you have been sentenced to death. Now you must die.' With that he fell back into the snow and began to snore harshly, while the two noncoms stared at his ashen, emaciated face in mute horror.

CHAPTER 6

A heavy silence had settled with the darkness over the battlefield. Here and there, the sudden angry chatter of a machine gun broke the silence, and routinely the German mortars on the other side of the river belched obscenely and another mortar bomb winged its way into the darkness to come howling down the next instant. Now and again, flares shot into the sky, illuminating the shattered ground for moments before diving down in a splutter of sparks like a fallen angel.

Cautiously, Hannemann and Slack-Arse, with de la Mazière trailing behind, attached to Hannemann by a length of rope, made their way towards the shot-up armoured vehicles, hugging the shadows, hardly daring to breathe at times, for the Slovak infantry were dug in on all sides. They could hear them quite plainly as they whispered together in the darkness, their teeth chattering in the freezing night cold. Silently they stole through the Slovak positions like grey ghosts.

They began to move between the shattered vehicles. They passed a shot-up troop carrier filled with dead soldiers, still sitting upright in their seats like rotting cabbage stalks in a winter allotment. They tripped over the bundles that had been infantrymen, already frozen stiff and rigid, each one caught in the moment of death, passionate and eloquent in their last, dramatic pose.

'Heaven, arse and twine,' Slack-Arse breathed, trying not to notice the stench of death, 'they put the wind up me all right. Shitting stiffs everywhere!'

'Knock it off,' Hannemann growled, tugging at the rope, 'or you'll be a shitting stiff your —' The words died on his lips. To his front something had moved!

As one they froze. Even de la Mazière ceased his low mumbling, as if the sudden danger had penetrated even his poor, disordered mind.

For what seemed an age, they crouched there among the dead, their hearts thudding, their nerves tingling with electric tension, straining their ears trying to identify the sound.

There it was again. This time there was no mistaking it: the soft pad-pad of a dog's paws on the surface of the frozen snow. A moment later Hannemann's nostrils wrinkled in disgust at the raunchy, animal smell of the hound.

'It's a mutt,' he whispered out of the side of his mouth. 'If it barks, Slack-Arse, we're shittingly well sunk.'

'What can we do?' Slack-Arse quavered. They were still a good hundred metres from the river bank and the Slovaks were all around them in the glowing darkness.

'Pray! Shittingly well *pray!*'

Suddenly Hannemann's heart skipped a beat. The dog had sensed they were there.

Silhouetted against the blood-red light of a flare, they could see the long-haired brute now, muzzle raised to the sky, nostrils twitching as it tried to identify the direction of their smell.

Gingerly, very gingerly, Hannemann let go of de la Mazière's rope and reached into the pocket of his tunic for his automatic, gaze fixed almost hypnotically on the animal as it poised there with its jaws open, saliva dripping and vicious toothed.

The dog moved. It had spotted them.

'Here it comes, Hannemann!' Slack-Arse whispered.

'I'm not fucking blind! Watch the Old Man. Run for it, if the balloon goes up.' He closed his mouth, crouched and waiting. The brute was heading straight for them.

At three metres' distance, the big dog — it looked as if it weighed all of a hundred pounds — stopped and let out a low throaty growl. Hannemann tensed. Suddenly the hand gripping the pistol was wet and sticky with sweat. He swallowed painfully and waited.

The hound went back on its powerful haunches, its wet upper lip curled upwards to reveal evil-looking yellow fangs. Hannemann knew the signs. In a moment it would spring. He raised the pistol butt, and prepared himself to bear the beast's weight.

'He —'

He never finished the words. In that same instant the hound launched itself into the air. It struck him full in the chest. In spite of his size Hannemann went staggering to his knees, nostrils suddenly full of the sickening animal stench. Blindly he smashed his butt down on the beast's sloping head. It avoided the blow easily and dripping saliva onto Hannemann's face, went for the NCO's throat.

Struggling wildly under the beast's weight, Hannemann tried to free himself and get in another blow. The hound's paw ripped savagely across his cheek. He stifled his yelp of pain just in time. Blood splattered the snow everywhere. The copper smell of warm blood seemed to turn the dog crazy. Growling low in its throat, it writhed and twisted furiously, trying to sink its fangs into the noncom's throat. Hannemann's face contorted with fear and disgust. He was swamped in the beast's nauseating, evil, rank smell.

'Get him off me,' he gasped. 'For God's sake, get the shitting bastard off me!'

But Slack-Arse seemed mesmerised. He was rooted to the spot, watching helplessly as man and beast writhed back and forth on the blood-stained snow, pistol dangling loosely from his fingers.

Suddenly de la Mazière woke out of that crazy trance of his, and flung himself on the animal's twisting turning back. He jammed one elbow between the hound and Hannemann's face beneath. Immediately the dog sank its fangs into de la Mazière's flesh. He did not seem to notice. Thrusting his arm ever deeper into the dog's mouth, his other hand sought and found what he was looking for: the hound's weak point — its genitals. He squeezed. The animal's spine arched with agony. He pressed his arm deeper into the hound's mouth, stifling its howl of pain. Remorselessly, ruthlessly, gasping with the effort, the sweat now streaming down his haggard face, he increased his fierce grip, squeezing harder and harder. The dog went on to its haunches. He held on. It tore its head to left and right, trying to free itself. Grimly, chest heaving crazily, de la Mazière fought back.

The battle seemed to go on for ever until Hannemann suddenly hissed: 'For shit's sake, Slack, brain it one!... Hit it, *mensch*!'

At last, while de la Mazière still held on, gasping for breath like an asthmatic in the throes of a fatal attack, Slack-Arse Schmidt began to rain blows onto the beast's great skull. Blood sprayed them all. Bone splintered and cracked. But still the dog fought back, though its struggles were getting progressively weaker. Again and again, Slack-Arse smashed the butt of his pistol down onto the hound's skull. Now the head felt like jelly, a rubbery slippery red mess. Yet it still would not die.

'Croak, croak…' de la Mazière crooned, feeling his fingers gripping the animal's genitals beginning to stiffen, lose all feeling, go numb. Would the monster *never* die?

Then it gave one last heave. A sigh, almost sad and forlorn. Abruptly it was limp — and dead.

For one long moment de la Mazière hung on, not quite believing that the struggle was finally over. But it really was dead. Slowly, fingers wet and sticky with blood, he let go. The beast fell on one side in the crimson snow. They had slaughtered it.

Gingerly, in unconscious parody of someone stepping into a very hot bath, Hannemann put the tip of one foot on the ice, while the other two waited among the frozen bushes. To left and right of them the river bank was empty; and on the other side all was silent save for the chatter of a slow, heavy machine gun. Finally it seemed that the front was settling down for the night, the only enemy now the merciless cold.

Very carefully, Hannemann placed the full weight of one leg on the ice. It creaked, but that was all. He took a deep breath and with a conscious effort brought his other foot down. Now all two hundred pounds of his bulk were resting squarely on the ice. Again it creaked. 'It looks…' he said very slowly, as if reluctant to tempt the fates, 'as if it's gonna hold, sir.'

De la Mazière said nothing, but stared dully ahead, his face hollowed out to a red death's head in the light of a flare falling on the other side; he had relapsed once more into his strange, half-crazy mood of before.

'Well, if it can hold you,' Slack-Arse whispered, 'and that beer-gut of yours, it can hold anything, I suppose. What's the drill?'

'Spread out, two metres between each of us… Broken step, so that we're not placing too much pressure on the ice at one and the same time. Got it, sir?'

De la Mazière still did not respond, so Hannemann repeated what he had just said, speaking slowly and carefully, like one might to a small and not particularly bright child. Finally de la Mazière nodded.

'All right, you first, Slack —' began Hannemann.

'Why always me first?' Slack-Arse protested hotly, eyeing the black, gleaming stretch of ice apprehensively.

'Because rank hath its privileges. And because if you don't, I'll kick yer arse so hard that yer cock'll be hanging out of yer mouth instead of yer tongue!'

'Well, now, if yer put it like that, Hannemann…'

But Slack-Arse's sarcasm was wasted on the gigantic air gunner tonight. He was too apprehensive. He knew they could be discovered at any moment, here right in the middle of the frontline. If they were, it would be shoot first and ask questions afterwards. 'The Colonel will come in the middle. And you know why, Slack-Arse. I'll bring up the rear.'

'As the warm brother said to the Hitler Youth in the short—'

'Knock it off!' Hannemann interrupted him brutally.

'Don't fart about, man! Tuck yer hindlegs in yer back pocket, Slack-Arse, and move out.'

Slack-Arse said no more. Gripping his pistol more firmly in his right hand, he took his first tentative steps onto the ice, feeling his way gingerly, as if he were walking over egg shells, the frozen mass creaking alarmingly under his weight.

Hannemann waited a moment and then gave the CO a shove. 'Off you go, sir,' he hissed. 'Broken step, remember.'

Numbly de la Mazière stumbled after Slack-Arse while Hannemann looked on, shaking his head in dismay. Then it was his turn and he, too, stepped onto the ice.

They were on their way. This was the last stage of their long flight. The last survivors of the once famed 1st SS Stuka Wing were coming home.

Hannemann flung a final glance behind him. As far as he knew he was the last German soldier east of the River Ondava. For three long years, at the command of their Führer Adolf Hitler, the armies of the Third Reich had battled and bled for this accursed land. Now they had lost it for good. Boast as they might in Berlin, Hannemann knew they were fated never to return. The East was lost for ever. He shivered suddenly, as the sudden memory of all those young arrogant SS officers who had come to die in this place flashed before his mind's eye. Already their very graves were forgotten, as if they had never even existed. He shook his big head again and dismissed the poignant memory. Then he concentrated on the task in hand, the very personal business of saving one's skin...

The Sisters were as surprised as they were. Suddenly the two groups were facing each other in the glowing darkness, the three tattered fugitives and the heavy-set women partisans in their padded jackets, caught in the middle of one of their famed sneak raids on the German bank opposite. Even Red Rosa was too startled at first to react. For what seemed an age they stared at each other at ten metres' distance while somewhere to the right a machine gun chattered like an irate woodpecker, Red Rosa's monstrous bull's pizzle hanging limply at her side.

Surprising enough it was de la Mazière who acted first. '*Hit the dirt!*' he shrieked in a cracked voice. In that same instant, as the other two slammed down on the ice, he fired and yelled, 'Alarm! Alarm! ... *Partisanen!*' Next moment he had dropped to the ice himself.

The massed spandaus opened up instantly. Abruptly the left bank was ablaze with fire. Tracer zipped flatly across the ice towards the Sisters. De la Mazière, hugging the ice, could feel the heat of the bullets whizzing above his head. The gunners couldn't miss. Suddenly the trapped women were galvanised into frenetic hysterical action, whirling round and round under the impact of that merciless fire, arms and legs flailing crazily like puppets in the hands of a mad puppet-master.

Ilona went down to her knees, what looked like a handful of red jam thrown at her face, sobbing, 'Rosa ... help me, sister ... I'm blind ... I can't see ... Rosa.' She sank down among the rest of the heaped, twitching bodies.

Red Rosa herself slammed to the ice, a slug burning in her right calf as if a red-hot poker had just been thrust into the flesh, flailing the ice with her bull's pizzle in that first terrible agony. For a moment she froze there, surrendering to that overwhelming pain. But only for a moment. Suddenly she became aware of the danger she was in.

Desperately she began to edge her way over the frozen surface towards the other bank, the slugs cutting the air just above her head. She crawled, ears closed to the screams of agony, the death cries, the hysterical pleas for help from her Sisters, who had fought for her and loved her, abandoning their homes and families to follow her into the hell of partisan warfare, and to share her rough bed whenever she so desired.

'I *must* live,' she pleaded through gritted teeth, 'I *must* live... Let me live... The Soviet Motherland needs me more than them...' Again and again she struck the ice with the bull's pizzle, trying to beat away the cruel pain in her shattered leg that threatened to overwhelm her before she reached the safety of the other bank. 'I must live, I *must* —'

There was a sudden ominous cracking sound. But in her crazed determination to reach the other side, Red Rosa did not notice the warning. She crawled on, sobbing hysterically with pain and fear, like the silly women had sobbed afterwards when she had taken them at night in her usual rough manner.

'I *must* live,' she chanted to herself. 'I *must*!'

Beneath her heavy weight, the ice heaved and buckled. She struck it another angry blow, not understanding what was happening. Perhaps she fancied that the ice was trying to stop her reaching safety. Rapid crack lines ran to left and right, giving off little snapping sounds. The ice heaved and swayed even more.

Suddenly she felt ice-cold water seep into the knees of her thick trousers. She crawled on, shaking her head crazily, as if to ward off the inevitable. The bank was only metres away. She was going to do it … she was going to do it…

Now she was crawling through icy water, her hands wrist-deep in slush, the ice sliding away beneath her knees. '*No!*' she shrieked. 'Oh *no* — please, no…' She raised that monstrous knout one last time and whacked it down with her suddenly numb hand, using the last of her rapidly fading strength. The ice gave. She went in face-forward. One last shriek. The bull's pizzle fell from her hand. A shocked gasp. Then she was gone in a brief flurry of icy water … for good.

Thirty metres away, listening to the rapid crack and snap of the ice as it began to break up everywhere, de la Mazière sprang to his feet. '*Nicht schiessen!*' he cried. Desperately he waved his hands as a searchlight swung round and blinded him in its harsh silver light. 'Don't shoot — we're German! *Nicht schiessen!*' He waited no longer. The snap-crack was turning into a roar. 'Run for it! *Run for it, lads!*' he cried, as the firing started to die away and hoarse cries of warning came floating across from the German side to the three men still on the ice.

They needed no urging. They doubled forward over the heaving, tilting ice, springing over the writhing bodies of the dying women, going all out as great black cracks raced after them, already hearing their boots splashing through slush and water, arms working like pistons, breath coming in harsh, hectic gasps.

A minute later they were slamming, one after another, into the freezing mud of the opposite bank, their bodies in icy water up to the thighs, tears of joy streaming down their emaciated faces. Eager arms were helping them up, men were slapping them on their backs, honest German voices were welcoming them back from the dead, hands thrusting bottles of schnapps at them, hunks of bread and sausage, as they were submerged in the tongues and dialects of their native country.

They had done it. They were home. The last survivors of the 1st SS Stuka Wing had reported in.

CHAPTER 7

The Prague Senior Officers' Mess celebrated the First Advent. In the centre of the panelled room, a single candle burned on the holly wreath. From the radio came the Christmas carols of the Homeland. The long tables were laden with biscuits and cakes. Neat Czech waitresses, in black uniforms and frilly white aprons, hurried back and forth bearing trays of glasses filled with champagne. At the far end of the room, logs crackled merrily in the big open fire place. Snow was falling gently outside. It was the kind of picture-postcard Advent scene that all the elegantly uniformed SS officers and their prettily gowned ladies remembered from their youth. The war and all its suffering could have been a million kilometres away, instead of only fifty, further east in Slovakia. It was December 7th, 1944; and the war in the East was hopelessly lost.

'*Naturlich,*' Major Baron Karst was saying to a plump quartermaster colonel, whose sole decoration was the War Service Cross, Third Class, 'the situation in the East does not look particularly good at the moment. But you must remember, Colonel, that the night is always blackest just before the dawn.'

'Agreed,' the fat Colonel said hurriedly and clicked his fingers at a passing waitress. 'Champers, girl — at the double!' he barked in the clipped military tone he affected, although in reality he was merely an accountant in uniform. 'You chaps from the fighting front know a lot more than we — er, base stallions,' he chuckled, 'as I believe you — er — front swine tend to call us.'

Karst nodded patronisingly. He liked Prague and this rear echelon world where he was lauded and spoiled as the last survivor of the 1st SS Stuka, which had been destroyed so tragically in the East. He was in no hurry to ask for an active command. 'There are still the Führer's secret weapons,' he hinted darkly. 'We have seen just how much London has suffered from our V-1 and V-2. But they are just the start. Those Anglo-American air gangsters will soon learn what is —' He stopped short, his champagne glass almost tumbling from suddenly slack fingers, bottom lip dropping open with surprise.

The big oaken doors had been flung open to admit a blast of cold air. A tall emaciated figure with tragic eyes stood there, legs spread, machine pistol clenched in his ungloved hands, the skinny shoulders of his ragged stained uniform sprinkled with snow. Behind him two other tattered grey ghosts had posted themselves at each side of the steps, their Schmeissers levelled at the helmeted sentries threateningly.

For one long moment there was no sound in the great hall save the saccharine-sweet voices of the children's choir trilling the song of the Christmas tree: 'O *Tannenbaum, o Tannenbaum, wie grun sind deine Blatter...*' Suddenly a Czech waitress entered from the kitchen, pressing open the door with her plump black bottom. She turned, saw those three grim figures standing there so menacingly, shrieked and dropped the tray of glasses with a great bang.

It broke the spell.

Standing next to an abruptly ashen-faced Karst, the fat Colonel flushed angrily and demanded, 'What in three devils' name is this?... Who are these people, sentry?... What are they doing here?' He looked at the sentries who guarded the mess.

The sentries swallowed hard, their adam's apples jerking up and down their skinny throats, but said nothing. They could read the lethal menace in the eyes of these 'front swine' who had appeared so surprisingly out of the swirling snow and taken them by the short and curlies before they had been aware of what was happening to them.

The tall lean man ignored the Colonel. It was as if he did not see him, or any of that elegant throng of senior officers and their suddenly terrified women who clutched their escorts' arms in fear. 'Hauptsturmführer Baron Karst,' he rasped, iron in his voice, his eyes steely, 'you have been found to be a traitor and a coward … a coward who abandoned his comrades in the field. You know what the sentence is for cowardice in the face of the enemy — *death*!'

On all sides, the elderly staff officers gasped and a woman cried, 'Oh, my God, no!'

Karst's hand fell to his pistol holster.

The man at the door jerked the muzzle of his machine pistol up swiftly, his knuckles whitening around the trigger. Karst dropped his hand immediately, eyes bulging with terror. His lips trembled and he attempted to say something, head twisted to one side, as if he were choking, but no sound came.

'For God's sake, man!' the fat Quartermaster Colonel cried, knowing the situation looked highly dangerous, but as yet still sure of himself. 'I take it from your speech that you are an officer. Therefore you must surely know that you can't just burst in here like…'

The man at the door jerked the machine pistol from left to right. There was no mistaking the murder in his eyes now.

The fat Colonel stopped speaking and stumbled back out of range. All around him the others were doing the same, pushing and thrusting each other in their haste, dropping and trampling their glasses to fragments, while the Czech waitresses huddled protectively together, arms clasped around one another at the far end of the room.

Somewhere a woman began to sob with fear. A man said in a hushed voice, 'They're SS of course... Nothing more than wild animals, after being out there at the front all these years... Capable of any damned thing under the sun... Scum and killers, the whole black bunch of 'em believe you me.'

'De la Mazière,' Karst quavered, finding his voice at last. 'You don't understand. What happened at the airfield was a mistake, pure and simple. I had no other alternative but to make for our own lines ... honestly, that was all I could do.'

Colonel de la Mazière spat contemptuously on the polished wooden floor. 'You lie to the very end, Karst,' he snarled. 'Have you no spine whatsoever? A local counter-attack found one of those men you tricked into jumping over Russian lines. Before he died, he told the infantry what you —'

Karst had seen there was no hope for him. Suddenly he crouched, hand flashing to his holster once more.

Automatically de la Mazière pressed the trigger. The machine pistol chattered frantically at his side. The impact at such short range flung Karst against the wall of the bar. Bottles and glasses crashed to the ground. Behind him the mirror shattered into a gleaming spider's web, tripling the image of this final scene, as Karst, eyes full of disbelief that this was happening to *him*, stared down at the sudden line of red button holes stitched across the front of his elegant, bemedalled tunic. 'Detlev,' he croaked, blood trickling out of the side of his twisted mouth, 'I didn't mean —'

De la Mazière fired again. This time, unable to control the burning rage that threatened to overwhelm him, he kept his finger pressed hard on the trigger, systematically ripping Karst's body apart, flaying it like a butcher.

Karst's face disappeared in a welter of flying blood. Thick scarlet gobs of it splattered the wallpaper. Everywhere bits of shattered bone gleamed like ivory through the gore. De la Mazière ripped the bullets downwards. Karst's abdomen blew apart. His guts crawled out, steaming, like obscene hot sausages, and tumbled slowly between his sagging knees to the floor.

Still de la Mazière continued firing, carried away by that terrible primeval fury. Karst's flies burst. His genitals flipped out like yellow wax fruit. De la Mazière kept his finger on the trigger. The machine pistol chattered frenetically at his hip. The penis disappeared in a flurry of torn flesh and thick gore. The testicles followed a moment later. A dark velvet hole oozing blood and matter remained.

Still de la Mazière continued the systematic shredding of this thing that had once been a man, though Karst was already dead, supported there by the wall, bullet-pocked and splashed with bright red dripping blood. He ripped a burst down Karst's left leg and then the right. The flesh burst like an overripe fig. Scarlet matter, mixed with chips of bright white bone, erupted from the gaping hideous wounds. Still Karst continued to hang there against the wall, blood dripping from the whole length of that tortured flesh in awesome drops. And then it was over. The magazine was empty.

For one long moment de la Mazière continued to crouch there, Schmeisser tucked to his hip, eyes blank and unseeing, chest heaving as if he had just run a great race. Then he shook his head slowly, like a man trying to awaken from a deep sleep. He gasped, eyes suddenly full of disbelief at what he saw there: that scarlet, faceless horror slumped against the wall. The little machine pistol dropped from his nerveless fingers. He turned, shoulders bowed, and went out into the falling snow. Behind him Hannemann and Slack-Arse Schmidt closed the great doors solemnly. It was all over.

ENVOI

'The funny farm, sir?' Hannemann exclaimed as the wood-burning Berlin taxi started to plough its way up the snow-heavy drive, trailing black smoke behind it in a thick cloud.

'Yes — poor old Pegleg's celebrated funny farm, with the friendly fellows in white overalls,' de la Mazière said fondly, shaking his head at the memory.

'At least we're not arriving here in that rubber van the Major was allus talking about, sir,' Slack-Arse said, as they rounded a bend and the big secluded retreat came into view.

In front of them the ancient driver changed gear and nodded at the sign: *Military Hospital for Nervous Disorders.* 'Swing from the shitting chandeliers here, they do, like shitting chimps,' he grunted. 'Nervous disease, my arse. They're all shitting crackers up there.'

'Pity you ain't brought no peanuts with you to feed them with, then, fartmouth,' Hannemann snarled. 'The kind of money you're charging us for the pleasure of riding in this shitting contraption of yours, you could buy a whole shitting plantation!'

'These are hard times, sir,' the driver whined and braked to a shaky halt. Behind the taxi, the little trailer containing the wood-burning stove that powered the vehicle shimmied dangerously. 'Got to make a living the best yer can.'

Hannemann opened his mouth to say something, but de la Mazière shook his head and handed the driver a wad of dirty paper notes, not even bothering to count them. 'Here you are, grandad. Here's your fare.'

The driver looked at the money, which was the equivalent of a month's pay for the two sergeants. 'You ain't got no lung torpedoes?' he said. 'Or none of that good bean coffee you SS fellers get issued with, sir? I'd prefer it.'

Hannemann thrust up his middle finger and sneered, 'Sit on it, arse-with-ears — and I hope it makes yer eyes water!'

'No need to be common,' the taxi-driver grumbled as he pocketed the virtually worthless paper money and they got out.

'Come on,' de la Mazière said, already starting up the steps that led into the hospital.

'Shitting civvies,' Slack-Arse grumbled. 'Always shitting complaining! Just because the Amis and Tommies drop a few square eggs on 'em every day... Don't shittingly well know they're born yet.'

De la Mazière opened the door. His nostrils were immediately assailed by the familiar cloying smell of ether, urine and rotting flesh. Followed by the two noncoms he entered. To left and right the doors to the wards were opened. They glimpsed men in blue-and-white striped pyjamas everywhere, strapped up under complicated pulleys and gadgets, broken men swathed in yellow bandages, tubes leading to bottles beneath the white cots, stinking of fetid, wrecked flesh. Others sat on the beds, chatting and smoking, occasionally urinating into shallow bottles, the buxom young Red Cross nurses seeming not to notice. Then there were the completely broken ones, tossing and turning in their drug-induced sleep or sitting in corners, eyes empty, staring vacantly into space, crooning meaningless lullabies to themselves over and over again. They were the ones who would be kept hidden from German society for the rest of their days, until blessed Nature took its course and they would die.

'Second floor, they said,' de la Mazière said grimly and began to mount the stairs, the high-ceilinged hall echoing crisply to the sound of his boots.

Hurriedly the other two followed, with Hannemann muttering, 'That old shit in the taxi was right, Slack — there are some real old funny farm chimps in this place.'

Now they could hear the sound of a piano playing and riotous laughter. Someone was declaiming in a familiar voice, 'On the very threshold of victory, the German people will not capitulate to the imperialists but will, with the aid of the greatest popular rising of all time, brought about by such a mobilisation as history has never seen before, by the Home Guard —'

The Goebbels imitator, standing on a table in the centre of the smoke-filled crowded room, tunic ripped open at the collar, face flushed with drink, broke off suddenly as he spotted the three grim figures at the door.

'Oh,' he stuttered while his comrades clapped and egged him on to continue his impersonation, 'clap my arse in a sling — it's Obersturmbannführer de la Mazière!'

The noise died away at once as everyone turned to stare at the black-jacketed SS Colonel, guarded by the two husky noncoms with machine pistols slung across their burly chests. Everyone had heard of the SS Stuka ace who had slaughtered his second-in-command so brutally in Prague, and of how he escaped the death penalty at the eleventh hour only by personal intervention of the Führer himself. Hitler had even awarded him the 'diamonds' to the Knight's Cross, as a special token of his favour. Sudden unseen hands yanked the speaker down from the ward table. The red happy faces were abruptly solemn and apprehensive.

De la Mazière let them wait, as he stared around at them with his hard bitter eyes and twisted mouth, face set and cynical under his battered, rakishly tilted cap with its death's head badge.

It was an astonishing company who faced him. Germany's once famed and feared Stuka pilots, forcibly retired here to the 'funny farm' because they had lost their nerve, cracked up, wrecked too many planes due to battle fatigue, or simply lost any belief in final victory for the Third Reich. Now here they spent their days, hidden from the world, evading the depressing realities of day-to-day life in the Reich, drinking solidly from morning till night, trying to forget the fear of the inevitable end.

Slowly de la Mazière's lean face started to crack into a wintry smile. With his thumb he jerked his battered cap to the back of his cropped blond head and said softly, 'Relax, comrades, relax. I might be of the SS, but you know, comrades, I am one of you, too. A Stuka pilot... A jock riding one of those old crates.'

His words had a dramatic effect. The noise started up again as everyone started to talk. A Major with a Knight's Cross at his throat, handed him a glass of cognac. 'Pour that down your wing-collar, sir,' he said, using the familiar pilot's slang, 'it'll take the varnish off your tonsils!'

'Thank you, Major,' de la Mazière said, telling himself he was beginning to win them over already. He raised the glass in a toast and cried, '*Happy landings!*'

'*Happy landings, sir!*' they echoed as one and raised their glasses, too, overlooking the fact that the two noncoms at the door were not relaxing their hard-eyed vigilance for one moment, fingers still curling tightly around the triggers of their machine pistols.

With a quick gesture, de la Mazière flung his glass over his shoulder. It shattered against the wall. It was the kind of gesture they had all been accustomed to in the good old days, when they had still had their nerve, when their Stukas had been the Führer's 'flying artillery'.

'Right — so why am I here?' he asked, then answered his own question immediately. 'At the court-martial, my medical witness testified that I had been subjected to too much stress, that I'd seen too much combat. In other words, I should be sent to the funny farm, just like you have been for one good reason or another.' He looked around their suddenly solemn faces. 'But as you see, the Führer, in his infinite wisdom,' his voice was suddenly cynical at the mention of Hitler and his listeners took his point, 'thought I wasn't ready for the rest cure — just yet. I am here and I am still operational, commander of the 1st Stuka Wing once more.' He paused momentarily. 'But there is a catch, however, comrades. There are no more trained SS pilots available to fly my brand-new Stukas. They have all been sent to the front as infantry.'

Now the pilots were looking puzzled. What had the SS's problems got to do with them? They were all Luftwaffe officers.

De la Mazière told them. 'Now, comrades, I am ripe for the funny farm, so the bone-menders maintain … so why not find my pilots in that very same place?' He laughed suddenly.

Hannemann, standing by the door, noted a shade of hysteria in the laugh; it was the same sound he recalled from that long trek back to the River Ondava. Perhaps the Old Man was really cracked. But then — who *wasn't*, these shitting days?

'The insane leading the insane, comrades,' de la Mazière went on. 'A whole wing of flying madmen, eh? What better symbol of our glorious One Thousand Year Reich in this December of

1944!' He threw back his head and laughed again, as if the idea really amused him. 'Crazy men,' he gasped, 'flying a crate that is five years out of date, in an operation that only a crazy fat man like Hermann could dream up in the middle of one of his damned drug sessions!' Suddenly the laughter had vanished, and his face was lean and bitter once more. 'Yes, comrades — I am here to ask you ... *beg* you ... to join me for one last op.'

'One last op, Obersturm?' echoed the Major who had handed him the glass of cognac. 'An op using the Stukas — with this bunch of barnshitters and perverted banana-suckers flying them?'

'Yes, yes — tell us more about the op!' voices cried from all sides.

Now de la Mazière knew he had them; he had won them over. Crazy or not, these 'funny farm' pilots were still addicted to the heady excitement of the obsolete dive-bomber. It was to them what 'coke' was to that drug-sniffing monster, Fat Hermann.

He took his time before he sprang his final surprise, which would convert them wholly, if he was not mistaken. 'As you know, comrades, ever since those air gangsters the Anglo-Americans started large-scale bombing of our cities, Fat Hermann's reputation has taken a dive. It is said that the Führer no longer speaks to him. Now the Fat Man desires fervently to re-enter the limelight ... and we, comrades, plus all available fighter and bomber squadrons, are going to ensure that he does so. Or so he thinks.' He paused, straining to catch it... Yes, there it was, that old familiar sound. He had only a few seconds left now. 'A great new offensive is soon to be launched against the Anglo-Americans in the West.' He quelled the sudden burst of chatter with upraised hands. 'Through the Ardennes. Our part in that offensive, as conceived by the Fat

Man, is one huge surprise attack to knock out the whole of the enemy's air force in the Low Countries and Northern France. On the morning of January 1st 1945, comrades, our dear old Stukas will lead over one thousand.'

'*One thousand!*' someone breathed in awe at the number.

'Yes — one thousand aircraft, in the greatest air operation the Luftwaffe has staged since the good old days of 1940.'

Now the sound of that aeroplane engine was almost above the building. He hurried on.

'For one last time, comrades,' He shouted above the noise, 'we'll be the Führer's flying artillery again, in the van of the battle!… *Comrades, are you with me?*'

Their answer came back in a tremendous excited bellow, their faces flushed with that old remembered pride and fervent desire: '*Jawohl!… Jawohl, ja!…*'

Then there it was, flashing past the big window. As one, their faces full of sudden longing, they turned their eyes to the grey winter sky. Like a sinister black hawk it seemed almost to hover, all-conquering, infinitely beautiful in its sheer menace, the plane that had once held the whole of Europe in fear and trembling — the Junkers 87B, otherwise known as the 'Stuka'.

A NOTE TO THE READER

Dear Reader,

If you have enjoyed this novel enough to leave a review on **Amazon** and **Goodreads**, then we would be truly grateful.

Sapere Books

Sapere Books is an exciting new publisher of brilliant fiction and popular history.

To find out more about our latest releases and our monthly bargain books visit our website:
saperebooks.com

Printed in Great Britain
by Amazon